D0181110

INVISIBLE WOUNDS

Candace Walters

INVISIBLE WOUNDS

MULTNOMAH · PRESS

10209 SE Division Street, Portland, Oregon 97266 / 503 257-0526

Other **A Touch of Grace** books:
Becoming Complete
Empty Arms
Every Woman's Privilege
In the Name of Submission
A Time for Risking
Walking a Thin Line
With My Whole Heart
Women Under Stress

Unless otherwise marked, Scripture references are from the Holy Bible New International Version, copyright 1973, 1978, 1984, by the International Bible Society. Used by permission of Zondervan Bible Publishers.

Scripture references marked NAS are from the New American Standard Bible, © The Lockman Foundation 1960, 1962, 1963, 1968, 1971, 1972, 1973, 1975, 1977.

Edited by Liz Heaney
Cover design by Bruce DeRoos
© 1987 by Candace L. Walters

Published by Multnomah Press
Portland, Oregon 97266
Printed in the United States of America

All rights reserved. No part of this publication may be reproduced, stored in a retrieval system, or transmitted, in any form or by any means, electronic, mechanical, photocopying, recording, or otherwise, without the prior written permission of the publisher.

Library of Congress Cataloging-in-Publication Data

Walters, Candace L.
    Invisible wounds: what every woman should know about sexual assault/Candace L. Walters.
        p.   cm.
    ISBN 0-88070-218-4 (pbk.)
    1. Rape—United States. 2. Rape victims—United States-Psychology.   I. Title.
    HV6561.W35 1988
    362.8'8—dc19   87-32928
                                                               CIP

CONTENTS

TO THE READER

T oday in America rape has become a common occurrence. Thousands of daily acts of sexual violence throughout the country have created a climate of fear and intimidation. The threat of rape hangs over every female for her entire lifetime, affecting many of her movements.

Yet for all the publicity surrounding rape, few people have any accurate understanding of the subject or know how to help themselves or someone else confronted with the crime. This confusion is especially prevalent in the Christian community.

Adding to the confusion is the erroneous thinking that rape is a problem only for those outside the church. This mistaken belief leaves Christian women particularly vulnerable. It also leaves the woman who has been sexually assaulted, Christian or not, without help from an invaluable resource—the church.

These observations were confirmed by my years of rape crisis counseling, speaking to community groups on rape awareness and prevention, and writing articles on rape for Christian magazines. Hundreds of women (and some men) have spoken or written to me about their own or a friend's victimization. Many were similar to this woman's letter:

> I was a Christian and a virgin when I was raped. Everyone turned their backs on me, even my parents. I was treated like I was a criminal. My fiancé said I must have deserved it. I know God is always with me, but right now I have never felt so alone.

Some of these heroic survivors of rape have told their stories to me in depth. Five of these women, desiring to spare others the struggles they went through, have permitted me to write about them in this book. While their names have been changed to protect their privacy, the other details of their assaults and recoveries are true.

I agree with many experts who feel that the word *rape* has been too narrowly defined. Traditionally it has meant only forced intercourse by a man against a woman (except his wife). Today the definition has broadened, and has become law in many areas, to include every kind of forced sexual behavior. From a victim's point of view, an attempted rape or any nonconsenting sexual contact involving the hands, mouth, or a foreign object can be just as violating as a completed genital rape. Therefore, we increasingly hear terms such as sexual violence, sexual assault, and sexual aggression, which are used in this book.

The definition of rape has also broadened to include marital and male rape. While this book is written especially for females victimized by strangers or acquaintances, this is not meant to imply that the rape of men and the rape of wives by their husbands does not happen or is not as serious. While these two types of rape are only briefly mentioned in this book, the prevention tips, reactions, and recovery process are similar for all forms of rape.

I am always interested in seeing people's responses when they learn I wrote a book on rape. Many were encouraging, but more were shocked that I would want to tackle such a depressing topic. I answered the curious patiently. (Yes, I am using my real name. No, my husband is not mentioned in the book. Yes, my children knew that I was writing it—in fact both of my teenagers have given talks on date rape at their schools.) The more unusual the questions, the more it was confirmed to me that most people needed a more factual perception of sexual violence.

For too long, the woman who has been raped has been ignored, or treated as scandalous or sensational. She needs to be recognized as an individual victimized by a serious crime more than someone who has suffered a heinous experience. She deserves the most empathetic and educated response society—and the church—can offer.

I want to make rape a *speakable* crime and, for the victim, a respectable crime.

Acknowledgments

I am thankful for many people who supported me while I wrote this book. The most supportive was my husband, Jim, and our three children, Scott, Amy, and Toby, who gave me the extra time and solitude (and never complained about home-delivery pizza) needed to complete this project

I am indebted to Dr. Sherwood Wirt and the members of the Christian Writers' Guild of San Diego County, especially Judith Dupree's critique group, for their encouragement and professional guidance.

Julie Cave, a special friend and fellow writer, first urged me to attempt this book and then cheered me on until it was finished.

I am also grateful to my editor, Liz Heaney, and to the staff at Multnomah Press for agreeing to address this disquieting subject and for their expertise in publishing it.

Finally, my heartfelt gratitude to all the women who graciously allowed me to write about their own tragedies in order to bring hope and healing to others similarly wounded.

The damage that rape does is invisible; it doesn't leave marks on the body as much as it leaves marks on the mind and the soul.

Py Bateman

Problems call forth our courage and our wisdom; indeed, they create our courage and our wisdom. It is only because of problems that we grow mentally and spiritually. . . . It is through the pain of confronting and resolving problems that we learn.

M. Scott Peck

"I Never Thought It Could Happen to Me"

THE WOUNDED

No one likes to think about the possibility of being raped. We all tend to believe that rape is something that happens to other people. Some of us find it difficult even to say the word *rape*.

Many women fear the crime of rape more than any other of life's tragedies. It's the horror they hear about and think they would never survive—so they put it out of their minds either resigned to the inevitability of rape or convinced it could never happen to them. These paralyzing attitudes keep women unprepared for an actual assault and lead them to believe the situation is unchangeable.

The following five women know what it is like to be taken unaware by this sudden, horrifying, violent experience. They have courageously shared their stories throughout this book to help others be better prepared than they were and learn that the fear of rape is manageable.

"I Didn't Know What to Do"

"The most frightening time for me was immediately after the rapist left," said Barbara Blake, who was attacked in a parking lot near her apartment. "During the assault, I was mostly numb to what was happening. Afterward I didn't know what to do. I wanted to go home, but I was afraid the rapist would follow me, so I just started knocking on strangers' doors in my apartment building. I was becoming frantic because nobody answered. Probably because I looked so bad; my clothes were rumpled, I was mussed and dirty, and walked with difficulty. Finally someone called the police."

Barbara is short and soft with trim gray hair. A graduate of two Bible colleges, she served as a secretary and missionary in the Far East for many years. She was spending her retirement years in the Northwestern United States, where the rape occurred. Nothing in her upbringing or employment prepared her for the possibility of being sexually assaulted.

The day that Barbara was attacked, she was walking the two blocks from a store to her home. She was carrying a bag of groceries in one hand and in the other she held a cane to support her fractured ankle which was in a cast. Her assailant tripped her in the parking lot and then forced her to go with him to some bushes nearby. Barbara started struggling and screaming, but the man said he would use a gun on her if she continued to resist. He escaped after telling her not to call the police, and was never apprehended.

Barbara was fifty-seven years old at the time. Her recuperation was complicated in a number of ways. Since people commonly believe that only young, seductive women are victims,

Barbara was afraid her report would be met by skepticism. She didn't fit the stereotype. Also, because of the social values of her generation and since she had never been married, she found it particularly difficult to relate the sexual details of the rape to the authorities. Her physical healing took longer because of health problems already present, and her body was more susceptible to injury than that of a younger woman. Finally, the independence which she had worked so hard to achieve was shattered, yet she felt unable to move from the area where the attack occurred.

For many years Barbara had copied down scores of old hymns, many no longer in print, in a notebook. She knew most of the songs by heart. "The hymns that I had memorized were a source of comfort after the rape. Whenever I heard noises in my apartment at night, or had to pass by the place where I was attacked, or saw someone who looked like the rapist, or dozens of other fearful situations, I would sing stanza after stanza until my panic subsided. Though I was unprepared in many ways for the rape, I felt God used my memorization of these scriptural truths set to music to literally give me a song in my darkest night."

"I HOPE OTHERS WILL HEAR MY STORY AND GET HELP"

As a young teenager, Cathy Campbell was raped by a policeman. Shortly after Thanksgiving, and without telling anyone, she had left home to visit her father in a nearby town who was hospitalized with cancer. After getting off the bus, Cathy wandered around the unfamiliar city for hours trying to find the hospital. Finally a policeman offered to help. She followed unsuspectingly as he took her to a filthy room in a dilapidated tenement where he sexually assaulted her.

Cathy lacked the maturity to deal with the rape. Her family lacked the knowledge to help her. They blamed her for leaving home without permission and urged her to forget the whole thing. The only person who might have been able to comfort Cathy was her father. Tragically, he died three weeks after the rape.

"I Never Thought It Could Happen to Me"

A year later, still distraught over the assault and her father's death, Cathy ran away from home. To survive on the streets, she was soon seduced into prostitution by a pimp. It was not long before she was raped again, this time by seven men. She spent two weeks in a hospital recovering from her injuries.

The next ten years sadly reflected the life of a confused, frightened, and wounded young woman. In her self-destructive lifestyle, Cathy overdosed on drugs more times than she can remember. She also slashed her wrists, had three nervous breakdowns, was institutionalized twice, joined a motorcycle gang, became involved in illegal activities, spent time in juvenile hall, and gave birth to a child as the result of a third rape.

"It's hard to believe I'm still alive after all I went through," said Cathy. "I know God spared my life on numerous occasions even before I had a personal relationship with him. I hope that other young rape victims will hear my story and get help long before I did.

"Sometimes I'm uneasy having others hear about the awful parts of my past. But I feel that the only way people are going to get an accurate perception of rape is for victims to speak out. I ignore my embarrassment by remembering how desperately I needed someone to understand and help me."

Cathy is a wife, mother of three children, and a nurse. While she has a special empathy for victims of sexual assault, she also lends her support to a variety of people with problems that she once had: single mothers on welfare, anyone addicted to drugs, alcohol, or food, women contemplating abortion, the mentally disturbed, and teenagers in juvenile hall.

"I WAS EMBARRASSED"

"The rapist left me in my dark bedroom with my mouth, hands, and feet tightly bound with duct tape," said Ellen Foster. "I had never felt so horrified and helpless. It took me about half an hour to struggle down my porch steps and hobble across the wet lawn to the house next door. By the expression on my neighbor's face, I knew I looked awful. I was too upset to tell him I'd been raped, so I said I was burglarized. I didn't tell anyone what actually happened until a week later when I was talking with a female detective.

"My overall feeling was embarrassment. I was embarrassed when my neighbor, who hardly knew me, tried to remove the duct tape from my hair and bruised body. I was embarrassed to be seen disheveled and incoherent. I was embarrassed that my rape eventually became so public."

Because of the circumstances, Ellen Foster's rape received national news coverage. She had been recently listed in a magazine as one of the ten most eligible women in a large midwestern city. The annual feature selected and recognized single, successful, career women. Ellen was head percussionist for a major city symphony.

A convicted rapist recently released from prison saw the list and accepted a dare to rape all ten women. Ellen was the first woman he assaulted on the list. Within a month he had raped her and two additional women. The police then made the connection between the three victims and put the other seven frightened women under surveillance. The rapist was captured two weeks later, just before dawn, after cutting the window screen on the home of his intended fourth victim.

I met Ellen two years after her rape. She told me why she is so open about her assault. "It was unbelievably devastating, but gradually I found there is hope in the worst of circumstances. I discovered that I could survive, that I could keep it from destroying my life, and that I could help others by sharing what had happened to me. Rape must be discussed so that the victim can find help and healing."

"HARDLY ANYONE BELIEVED ME"

Ann Crawford is a pastor's wife and Bible study leader. She doesn't appear old enough to be the mother of three teenaged girls. When Ann and her daughters were on the "Family Feud" television program, the host, Richard Dawson, said they looked more like sisters.

"I Never Thought It Could Happen to Me"

Throughout high school and college, Ann was well-liked and a student leader. She also played competitive piano and was part of a Bible quiz team which won first place in the national finals. Nobody who knew Ann would have thought that a rape would be part of her future.

Ann's rape was different from Ellen Foster's in a number of ways. Ellen was raped by a stranger; Ann was raped by a trusted professional. Ellen's rapist was caught and imprisoned; Ann's rapist was never charged. Everyone believed Ellen's story; only a few people believed Ann's.

"I hesitated to tell anyone I was assaulted by my psychologist because hardly anyone was ever convinced it happened. Doctors are so highly revered, people can't conceive of one of them being a rapist. Naturally, since I was seeing a mental health professional, people thought I must have imagined that my therapist manipulated me into removing my clothes.

"He had been treating me for several months because I was depressed. I was so stunned by the assault that I paid the usual fifty dollars for the session, destroyed any physical evidence, and waited weeks to report it. Then the authorities said the case was too weak to prosecute. It would be my word against his and he was a church leader, a college professor, and a respected psychologist. Who would believe me?

"It is hard for any woman to say that she has been raped—there is such a stigma attached to it. It is even harder for a victim who is a Christian. For one thing, rape is rarely mentioned within the church. And secondly, if a woman does mention it, help within the Christian community is practically nonexistent. I don't know what I would have done without the strength I drew from my personal faith in God, but human support also would have helped tremendously."

Because her emotional support was minimal, Ann had a much more difficult time of recovery than Ellen did. Ann survived a suicide attempt and went through years of counseling before she reconciled the rape in her mind. While the news reported that Ellen's rapist was convicted and sentenced for his crime, the media featured Ann's rapist winning awards and gaining national recognition in the area of psychology.

"The Court Trial Was Devastating"

Elizabeth Green was raped by her neighbor. "He came over one afternoon to borrow some bread. While we were in the kitchen, he unlocked my back door so he could get in later that evening. When he returned, I was just going to bed and my three children were sleeping. He threatened to hurt them if I didn't cooperate. The rape was only the beginning of a nightmare with repercussions I never would have believed possible."

Elizabeth is a lovely, vibrant woman with an engaging smile. Her poise has been honed by years of professional singing. One wall in her home is lined with photographs and awards depicting her musical career. She speaks of the rape with regret, but not bitterness.

As in Ann Crawford's case, people couldn't believe Elizabeth could be assaulted by someone she'd known for months. "Basically, I had to start my entire life over after the rape. My marriage, already in trouble, quickly dissolved. I lost my best friend because she was the rapist's wife and didn't know what to believe. Rumors about me flourished, especially at church. I was asked to stop singing in the choir."

"The court trial was devastating. My bloody underwear and photos of my nude and battered body were used as evidence. Defense witnesses made me seem to be a wanton woman. And, even though three other women testified that they had also been assaulted by the same man, he got off with only six months in a treatment program for sex offenders. At times, I wondered whether it would have been better for me if I had never told anyone about the rape."

Elizabeth Green remarried several years after her rape. She and her husband sing together and often perform for various church and community functions. Sometimes Elizabeth will tell the story of her rape and recovery to an audience. "Even though it was hard for a while to believe that things would get better, I don't know how I would have made it through that period of my life without faith in God's unchanging love. Especially when hardly anyone else seemed to understand or care."

SEXUAL VIOLENCE: A FACT OF LIFE

Barbara, Cathy, Ellen, Ann, and Elizabeth are just five of the thousands of women who are victims of sexual violence each year in the United States. On the average, a woman is raped once every minute of every day.[1] According to the FBI, more than 84,000 women report being raped in a single year. Experts believe that if the women who are assaulted but do not report the crime were included, the figure would be more than one million rape victims annually.[2]

Sexual violence has become a fact of life in the eighties. The escalation of sexual assault is increasing at a rate that far exceeds population growth. Since 1933 the rape rate in America has increased over 700 percent, and experts say that this figure is conservative.[3] A survey taken by the 3M Corporation showed that in the 1940s the top three discipline problems in high school were chewing gum, running in the halls, and talking in class. Today the problems have escalated to theft, rape, and assault. Year after year, crime statistics show rape to be the most rapidly escalating violent offense. If this trend continues, the FBI estimates that one out of every four women will experience a rape or an attempted rape in her lifetime.

While most people think of a rapist as being unknown to the victim, marital rape and date or acquaintance rape is actually more common than stranger rape. Because of the silence surrounding spousal rape, few realize how often it occurs. Data from The National Clearinghouse on Marital Rape, a nonprofit organization in Berkeley, California, show that two million American women are raped by their husbands every year. Sociologists David Finkelhor and Kersti Yllo, authors of *License to Rape*, estimate that in the United States one in ten wives is raped by her husband.[4] Yet marital rape is the least reported, least believed, and most difficult to prosecute. In approximately half of our states, a man cannot be arrested for raping his wife if they are living together.

Second only to marital rape is date or acquaintance rape. Approximately half of all rape victims are attacked by someone they know. While adult victims over the age of twenty-five are more likely to be assaulted by a stranger, college-age females are mostly victimized by an acquaintance, in many instances within the context of a dating relationship.

A recent survey of 7,000 students at thirty-five colleges nationwide found that one in seven women reported being raped—47 percent by dates or acquaintances. The study, funded by the National Center for the Prevention and Control of Rape, also showed that one in every twelve men admitted to having fulfilled the prevailing definition of rape* or attempted rape, yet virtually none of those men identified themselves as rapists.[5] In another study, 35 percent of 6,000 college males questioned said they were likely to rape a woman if they could be sure of not being caught or punished.[6]

While the rape of men is far less common than the rape of women, emergency rooms and rape crisis centers across the country are seeing more and more men who have been raped by other men. While only 10 percent of female victims report being assaulted, it is felt that a much lower percentage of men report their victimization. Although there are no official statistics on male rape, some researchers say men account for 7-10 percent of all rape victims nationwide.[7]

The United States is considered one of the most civilized and compassionate countries in the world. Yet, in comparing crime statistics with those of eighty other nations, we learn that only three other countries report higher rape rates.[8] The figures on rape in the United States are much higher than other Western countries, between ten and thirty times higher than some European nations, for example.[9] Rape is nonexistent in many countries; in some cultures the very idea of rape cannot even be conceptualized.[10]

In marked contrast to its prevalence, the problem of rape is rarely discussed in educational literature. Secular and religious publishers have almost totally ignored the issue of sexual violence, yet there is no subject of such great importance affecting so many people that less has been written about.[11] However, outside the world of academics, the subject of rape is everywhere. Comedians, novelists, pornographers, and filmmakers have used rape scenes to entertain their audiences for many years.

---

* Every kind of forced sexual behavior.

21

During the past decade, increasing attention has been given to this major social concern. Since the 1970s, rape victim support groups have lobbied to educate the public, reform law enforcement, and rewrite legislation. While the nation's consciousness as a whole has been raised, individually people still view rape with misunderstanding, apprehension, or disregard. These kinds of attitudes often leave the survivor of sexual assault feeling alone, rebuffed, and without effective assistance.

Reluctance to understand rape has two sources: denial and ignorance. Rape is a depressing fact of life people prefer not to face, and in order to understand rape, most people have to dismiss everything they have already learned about it. The myths about rape have solid roots in ancient history. These misperceptions have remained with us into the twentieth century. Traditionally, society has remained passive to the plight of rape victims. Through direct and indirect means, the victim has been further victimized and the perpetrator has been protected. It is mainly through the testimony of courageous victims that we have any accurate understanding of rape at all.

Whether they realize it or not, rape and the fear of rape affect all women. It limits their freedom, inhibits their behavior, and influences the routes they walk and the hours they keep. In hundreds of ways, large and small, a woman must guard against the threat of an attack. Her chances of being victimized are greater than being in a car accident, getting breast cancer, or having a miscarriage.[12]

Yet most rape victims, along with Barbara, Cathy, Ellen, Ann, and Elizabeth, thought it could never happen to them. This refusal to face the possibility of rape greatly contributes to a woman's vulnerability. Women need more knowledge about why rape occurs, when they are more at risk, how to recognize a potential rapist, and what help is available for victims.

Rape recognition and preparedness might rob us of our taken-for-granted feelings of safety, but it doesn't make us any more susceptible to rape than doing a breast self-examination increases the risk of getting cancer or wearing a car seatbelt makes us more apt to have a collision. On the contrary, it adds to our protection and helps us lead healthier and safer lives. While knowledge of rape might force us to adjust our lives to the reality of rape, it can also lessen the intimidation the crime has traditionally induced. Awareness can help us to stop living in the shadow of our fears.

1. Linda E. Ledray, *Recovering from Rape* (New York: Henry Holt & Co., 1986), p. 9.
2. Helen Benedict, *Recovery* (Garden City, N.Y.: Doubleday & Co., 1985), p. 12.
3. Jerry R. Kirk, *The Mind Polluters* (Nashville, Tenn.: Thomas Nelson, 1985), p. 52.
4. David Finkelhor and Kersti Yllo, *License to Rape* (New York: Holt, Rinehart, & Winston, 1985), p. 7.
5. Ellen Sweet, "Date Rape," *Ms. Magazine,* October 1985, p. 56.
6. Elizabeth Kaye, "Was I Raped?" *Glamour,* August 1985, p. 258.
7. Benedict, p. 153.
8. David Wallechinsky, "We're Number One," *Parade Magazine,* September 21, 1986, p. 4.
9. Finkelor and Yllo, p. 248.
10. Kathryn M. Johnson, *If You Are Raped* (Holmes Beach, Fla.: Learning Publications, 1985), p. 17.
11. Andra Medea and Kathleen Thompson, *Against Rape* (Garden City, N.Y.: Doubleday & Co., 1974), p. 14.
12. Figures based on National Safety Council: 1 in every 8 people involved in an automobile accident; American Cancer Society: 1 out of every 10 women will develop breast cancer; American College of Obstetricians and Gynecologists: 1 in every 5 pregnancies ends in a miscarriage.

If victims can be seen as less competent, less strong, less smart, essentially less human than other people, a person who has not been victimized can feel immune to victimization.

Morton Bard and Dawn Sangrey

I'm beginning to feel like the untreatable, untouchable me with some kind of plague. It seems like nobody cares, just so they don't have to be the one to help.

Letter from a rape victim

"Doesn't Anybody Understand?"

THE INJURY

The man who assaulted Ellen Foster broke into her house while she was at orchestra rehearsal. While waiting for Ellen to come home that evening, he amused himself by playing with her large collection of musical instruments. He also unscrewed the lightbulb in her bedroom. After his arrest, he admitted to a policeman that as he crouched in the darkness, he had planned how he would humiliate, violate, and punish a woman he had never met.

Within a few hours Ellen changed from a confident young

woman into a bewildered individual who sometimes cried for hours; from a self-sufficient professional into someone incapable of living alone. One day Ellen was principal percussionist for a major city symphony, the next she had difficulty remembering music she had played for years.

Ellen's reactions were normal for a woman who has been sexually assaulted. Because neither she nor her family and friends could understand what was happening to her, it took two years before she began to feel normal again.

Yet Ellen Foster is an unusual survivor of rape. While most women prefer anonymity, she has gone public with her experience. She told why: "I was picked at random by a stranger to be tortured and defiled through no fault of my own. Others I know have been punished way out of proportion for making some small mistake, such as forgetting to lock a door or trusting the wrong person.

"Many times it is not only the rape that devastates a woman; it is the reaction of others who hear what happened to her. Most victims remain silent or anonymous because they rightly fear they will be misunderstood or judged. Fewer than one out of every ten rapes is reported to the police, and thousands of women live their whole lives without ever telling anyone.

"So few people understand what rape is or have learned how to deal with it if it happens to them or to someone they know. That's why a rape victim is treated with continuing injustice by nearly everyone, even herself. I'm willing to go public with my story to try to change that cycle of injustice. We cannot always prevent rape, but we can have more control over our recovery from it."

Despite widespread media attention, reformed laws, and increased sensitivity, sexual assault remains an ambivalent issue in most people's minds. More often than not, the rape victim is seen as less than human. The sympathetic consider her pitiful or disturbed. The unsympathetic see her as promiscuous or contaminated. It seems as if everyone is ashamed for her. Unlike any other victim of a violent crime, she is categorized as stupid or as a failure for getting raped. People forget that rape is caused by the rapist—not the victim.

These attitudes and the lack of concern for survivors of sexual violence are perpetuated by numerous myths. Five main myths are largely responsible for the rape victim's slow, sometimes non-existent recovery.

MYTH: RAPE IS SEXUAL ACTIVITY

At the root of the other myths is the misbelief that rape is sex. Most people mistakenly think of rape as violent sex rather than sexual violence. While the mechanics of rape are sexual, the primary motivation is violence. *Rape is aggression that is acted out sexually, not sex that is acted out aggressively.*

Numerous studies show that the main objective of the rapist is to dominate, control, and devalue his victim. Rape is a pseudosexual act in which the offender uses sex to vent feelings of anger, inadequacy, and frustration.[1] Sexual behavior becomes the channel for expressing and discharging hostility, not sexual needs.

A look at the four main types of rapists shows this to be true. Ellen Foster's assailant was twenty-six years old. He had been in and out of jail for burglary and rape since the age of sixteen. A court psychiatrist, after examining Ellen's rapist, said he represented the most common type of rapist, usually classified as a *power rapist*. He is a man who sees himself as inferior and a failure. He rapes so he can have status and significance, not for a sexual outlet.

His assaults are usually premeditated and follow a particular pattern. Interviewed in prison by a news reporter, this short man with missing front teeth boasted about making love to attractive, successful women: "I gave them something they wanted."

The second most common type is the *anger rapist*. As the name implies, this man is furious at some person or situation in his life and he rapes for revenge. His attack is often impulsive and violent, triggered by an insult or conflict. He feels he has been wronged or unjustly humiliated, so he rapes to get even. The victim may be the actual object of his anger or a convenient substitute. The anger rapist is usually more brutal and forceful

27

than the power rapist as he releases his rage physically. Many of these men have been victims themselves of physical or sexual abuse.[2] They may be re-enacting or retaliating for their own traumatic experiences.

The third type, the *sadistic rapist*, is the rarest kind even though the news media have given him the most publicity. He finds sexual gratification in ritualistic torture of his victim; it often results in homicide. The aggression of the offender becomes eroticized so that he derives pleasure from hurting someone, whether or not actual sexual contact is made. Such a man has learned to associate sex with violence, frequently through exposure to pornography, and cannot become sexually aroused unless violence is involved.[3]

It is generally agreed that the offenders in the fourth category, *men or boys who rape as groups*, are motivated somewhat differently than the solitary rapist. Gang rape is a way for a group of men to achieve recognition, show off, or develop cohesiveness. They do it as a ritual signifying manhood or as a means of ostracizing others who won't participate. Gang rape is not an assault by a number of rapists but rather by a group that rapes. Psychologically, the man who rapes with a group is considered to be less perverted than the lone offender because his motivation is not primarily power or anger, but to prove his masculinity to his peers. Most gang rapists wouldn't initiate a sexual offense unless they were in a group situation. It is unlikely that they will have a criminal record as a sex offender.[4]

Cathy Campbell remembers her gang rape as a sort of contest between her seven assailants. After each man finished with her, the group challenged another to participate, cheering him on as if it were a competitive sport. While Cathy lapsed in and out of consciousness, the men partied, joked, and slapped each other on the back. It was only because the group was more concerned with interacting with each other than with Cathy that she was able to get away.

While most rapists have a mixture of these four motives, they are dominated by one. None, however, are primarily motivated by sexual desire. Rape is first and foremost an act of violence which usually causes physical as well as psychological harm to its victim.[5] It is usually a desperate act of an insecure and emotionally dysfunctional individual who is unable to handle the stresses of his life.[6]

People who view rape as sexual activity rather than sexual violence believe that the rapist is motivated by uncontrollable desire, that the woman is somehow responsible for the attack, and that rape does not hurt the victim any more than sex does. They reason that it is not a cause for concern, but a subject to shun or to snicker about.

A sex crime specialist with the San Diego Police Department said, "Rape is no more related to sex than being beaten over the head with a bat has something to do with the game of baseball. The use of sexual organs does not make rape a sexual act. Rape is a violent act in which sex is used as a weapon to inflict pain. It should be classified as a crime of kidnapping, assault and battery, unlawful imprisonment, and attempted murder. Not as a sex crime."

MYTH: BAD WOMEN PROVOKE RAPE

When rape is seen as sex and the rapist is thought to be driven by uncontrollable passion, this naturally leads to the myth that the victim somehow enticed him; therefore, only sluttish women are raped. But sexual assault is almost never committed out of lust. Every woman and child is a potential victim. A rapist in prison wrote, "The victims are not to blame, it's all my fault. I'm the one with the problem, not her. She was just in the wrong place at the wrong time. I don't even know her name. I'd never seen her before." *The most important reason women are targeted by a rapist is their vulnerability, not their sexiness.*

The age, attractiveness, size, color, or morals of a woman have very little to do with her being singled out, except if a particular characteristic reminds the offender of someone he loathes. A serial rapist in California chose women in their nineties because they represented an authority figure to him. Another man suddenly attacked a woman who was driving the same kind of car as his mother, whom he despised. Some assailants boast that they are doing unattractive women a favor by assaulting them. Others, such as Ellen's rapist, say they rape men as well as women; gender makes no difference to them.

Rape is the only violent crime that absurdly implies the victim was at fault. We would never think of asking the victim of a hit-and-run accident what he was doing in that part of town or asking a burglary victim why he tempted his assailant with such an attractive television set. It is preposterous to think that a woman would do anything to provoke a physical attack that risks venereal disease, pregnancy, emotional trauma, injury, mutilation, or even death.

MYTH: WOMEN ARE RAPED BY STRANGE MEN IN DARK ALLEYS

Most people think a rapist is an ugly, seedy, demented loner who lurks in dark alleys and deserted parking lots, waiting for his prey. While a few do meet this description, most do not. There are no obvious physical features that would point out a rapist.[7] The impulse to rape is not connected to a man's appearance, age, income, education, or status. He may be a teenager or a grandfather, a church member or an atheist, a college graduate or a high school dropout.

What kind of men rape women? Although there is a broad assortment of individual differences in rapists, there *are* some common characteristics. The man who rapes usually has a poor self-image, a distorted view of sexuality, difficulty establishing and maintaining intimate relationships, and trouble coping with frustration. He is, for the most part, insensitive or indifferent to the feelings of others and seeks immediate gratification without concern for the consequences.[8] While the sex offender has a serious behavioral problem that needs to be treated, he may appear normal in some areas of his life. Some hold respectable, responsible jobs, and many are married and have children—a woman would have no reason to mistrust them initially. In more than half of all reported rapes, however, the victim knows or is known by the perpetrator.[9]

Studies of convicted rapists show that as many as 75 percent plan ahead to commit rape. Some plot with a definite female in mind, watching her for weeks to learn her personality, schedule, and the routes she takes from place to place. With this information he can determine when and where she would be most vulnerable to attack. Other rapists are motivated simply by the idea of rape; their victim will be any unprotected and vulnerable woman they can find. Sex offenders can become experts at judging a woman's vulnerability by observing her walk, dress, speech, and behavior.

Rapes do take place on dead-end streets and isolated areas, but they also occur indoors. The most likely place for an attack is in a woman's own home. Other frequent locations are automobiles, the assailant's home, or buildings open to the public. No environment is safe.

MYTH: WOMEN FALSELY ACCUSE MEN OF RAPE

Society's blind fear of the vindictive, untruthful woman was reinforced in 1985 when Cathleen Crowell Webb said she lied during her rape trial which sent Gary Dotson to prison six years earlier. In actuality, a woman's chances of convicting a guilty man, let alone an innocent one, are minimal. Even Mrs. Webb admits that it was not her lie that convicted Dotson, but rather a faulty legal defense.[10]

Rapists are more successful than any other criminal in getting away with their crimes. It is not uncommon for a man to have committed twenty or thirty sexual attacks before he is caught, identified, charged, and prosecuted. The average rapist attacks about once a week and many as often as three times a week.[11] The police make an arrest in less than half of all reported rapes (as compared with about 80 percent of all homicides). The odds are about even that the case will never come to trial, and if it does, the defendant is just as likely to be acquitted as convicted. Of those convicted, two out of five will plea bargain for a lesser offense.

It is rare for a woman to report a rape that has not happened. It is more likely that she has not reported a rape that

31

has happened. Even a victim who recants may not have lied about being raped; she may have decided to change her story for a variety of reasons such as her family has been threatened by the rapist or her memory of the rape is partially blocked or she fears publicity.[12]

FBI statistics show that false accusations for rape are the same as for any other felony, less than 3 percent. Every woman who decides to prosecute must undergo an extensive medical exam, a thorough interrogation by the police, and a detailed court testimony. One district attorney involved in hundreds of rape cases says it is nearly impossible for a false accusation to come to trial, and we should be more concerned with protecting the victim's rights, not the rapist's.

MYTH: RAPE DOESN'T CONCERN ME

Denial will not make rape go away, it only makes it worse. Our apathy helps create a climate where sexual assault is tolerated and the victim is isolated because we ignore the extent and seriousness of the problem. Rape is an affront to every civilized human being, and spreads its consequences into all of society.

Since it is estimated that 25 percent of all women will be assaulted and 7-10 percent of all rape victims will be men, it is probable that most people, even if not victimized themselves, will have a friend or a loved one become a victim. If all forms of sex offenses, including lewd conduct, indecent exposure, obscene behavior, and molestation of minors, were figured in these estimates, nearly everyone would be listed as victims.

OTHER MYTHS ABOUT RAPE

Hundreds of other myths have obscured the truth about rape. Some of the more common ones are:

Myth: Rape is a biological necessity.

Fact: Men are not motivated to rape by some uncontrollable biological urge. If that were true, then all men in all cultures would rape. Rape is a learned behavior taught by attitudes, environment, and values of individuals and society.

Myth: Women secretly want to be raped.

Fact: Fantasy is not reality. Many people daydream about things they would never want to actually happen. It may be true that some women have sexual fantasies in which varying degrees of force play a part, but these thoughts are unrelated to wanting to be an unwilling victim of a violent, nonsexual criminal act.

Myth: It is not possible to rape a woman without her consent.

Fact: It is possible to rape a nonconsenting adult. Many woman react with paralyzing fear when physically attacked. The fear of death or threat of brutality can immobilize anyone.

Myth: If a woman is not physically injured, it was not rape.

Fact: More than half of all rape victims are too intimidated or frightened to use physical resistance. They may choose to submit rather than risk serious injury or death. The wounds to a woman's spirit are more serious and prolonged than the visible trauma.

Myth: Most rapes are interracial.

Fact: Like most other crimes, the majority of rapes are intraracial. Nine out of ten sexual assaults involve persons of the same race or culture.

Myth: There is no way to protect oneself against rape.

Fact: There are numerous ways to reduce the risk of being raped. The refusal to face the fear of rape is one of the major reasons why a woman is vulnerable to attack. The rational woman deals with that fear and takes steps to minimize the danger.

PUBLIC HELP AND ACCEPTANCE NEEDED

Rape remains one of the most ill-defined and misunderstood words in the English language. Because victims—the real experts on rape—have usually remained silent out of embarrassment, fear, or ignorance, people's opinions have been formed by other sources. These sources consist of television, movies, novels, music, jokes, and offhand remarks, all of which frequently perpetuate and intensify fallacies about rape.

People resist changing their false conceptions. The myths make them feel safe. Myths allow us to believe that rape really does not happen that often and if it does, the woman could have prevented it. Myths foster a feeling of control over our own lives. They help maintain our belief that if we are good people and do the right things, bad things will not happen to us. Unfortunately, this attitude is especially prevalent in the Christian community because we often feel that God protects his followers from harm.

For too long rape has thrived on these misconceptions, our own prejudices and indifference, and the silence of its victims. Ellen Foster is telling her story on television, at public gatherings, and on the printed page because she wants to see these myths dispelled and the silence broken. "Everyone must realize that, as hideous as rape is, it becomes worse if the victim thinks it is unspeakable and insoluable. The Christian community especially needs to make an impact in this area. Secular groups do not understand the need for God's supernatural power in dealing with the aftermath of a sexual assault. I think it is essential for complete recovery. Rape can be the worst thing to happen to a woman, but it doesn't have to be. With public acceptance and proper help, a rape victim can recover completely."

1. A. Nicholas Groth and H. Jean Birnbaum, *Men Who Rape* (New York: Plenum Press, 1979), p.2.
2. Linda E. Ledray, *Recovering from Rape* (New York: Henry Holt & Co., 1986) p. 201.
3. Marie Marshall Fortune, *Sexual Violence: The Unmentionable Sin* (New York: The Pilgrim Press, 1983), p. 179.
4. Ledray, p. 199.
5. A. Nicholas Groth and H. Jean Birnbaum, *Men Who Rape*(New York: Plenum Press, 1979), p. 12.
6. Ibid, p. 5.
7. Helen Benedict, *Recovery* (New York: Doubleday & Co., 1985), p. 9.
8. G. Keith Olson, *Counseling Teenagers* (Loveland, Colo.: Thom Schultz Publications, 1984), p. 442.
9. Alan W. McEvoy and Jeff B. Brookings, *If She is Raped* (Holmes Beach, Fla.: Learning Publications, 1984) p. 29.
10. Cathleen Crowell Webb and Marie Chapian, *Forgive Me* (Old Tappan, N.J.: Fleming H. Revell Co., 1985), p. 219-20.
11. Dorothy Hicks et al., *Everywoman's Health* (Garden City, NY: Doubleday & Co., 1980), p. 368.
12. Ledray, p. 13.

People in trouble have to overcome three difficulties: their problem, whatever it is; their "natural" reluctance in this society to accept the identity of a needy person; and the indifference of the systems that are supposed to help them.

Morton Bard and Dawn Sangrey

It is so much easier to tell a person what to do with his problem than to stand with him in his pain.

David Augsburger

3

"Where Do I Go for Help?"

FIRST AID

I n the middle of one of my twelve-hour night shifts as an on-call crisis counselor, I heard a woman identifying herself as an emergency room nurse at a local hospital. It took me a few seconds to realize that I had picked up the ringing phone in my sleep.

"The police are bringing in a twenty-two-year-old rape victim named Laura. They will be here in thirty minutes. She needs someone to stay with her through the evidentiary exam."

My bedroom was dark. I focused on the neon clock numbers on the nightstand. They read 3:19. While listening for the hospital's location and the victim's circumstances, I sat up to clear the sleep from my mind.

"I'll be there as soon as I can." My words sounded glued together.

I hurriedly dressed in jeans, a sweater, and tennis shoes. While I waited for the microwave oven to heat water for coffee, I told my husband where I was going and called my supervisor at the Rape Crisis Center. In the car I carefully locked all the doors and fastened my seatbelt, grateful that the gas gauge read half full. I played the radio loudly on the nearly deserted freeway to erase my sleepiness and keep me company.

When I arrived at the hospital, I pulled into the parking space closest to the entrance in the empty lot. The emergency room was vacant except for a man mopping the floor. The smell of disinfectant was strong. I was briefed by a tired nurse who was about to go off duty and by a Sergeant Anderson who brought Laura in.

I went to the examining room and introduced myself to Laura. She fidgeted on the hard examination table, trying to keep the immodest blue hospital gown from revealing too much. Her long, brown hair was tangled and matted to a scrape on her forehead.

"Do you want to call anyone, Laura?" I asked after carefully closing the sliding partition.

"No," she sighed. "I moved here only last month. My parents live in another state and my father's not well. I don't want to upset them right now. I'll call them when things settle down."

"Okay, I'll do what I can for you. If you have any questions or don't understand why you are being asked certain things, you can stop the doctor at any time. The examination for evidence might not be pleasant, but it should not be painful. The pelvic exam will probably be the worst part. If you can try to relax and hold my hand if you want to, we'll get through this together." I watched Laura to make sure she understood what I said and wished for another system that would spare her further distress.

As I talked with Laura and read the police report, I was able to piece together Laura's story.

She had been alone in the laundry facility of her apartment complex that Friday evening. She had locked the door with her key. Most of the other young, single tenants were gathered in the recreation room for the monthly get-together, but she had declined to join them. Last month's party had been too wild for her tastes.

She could hear the music from the party above the noise of the two washing machines. She was bent over, concentrating on removing a stain from her blue silk blouse. She did not hear the laundry room door unlock, nor did she realize that anyone had entered the room until a hand was roughly clamped over her mouth and a coarse voice growled, "Don't scream or I'll cut that pretty face of yours."

After Laura's assailant raped her, he hit her head with the blunt end of a knife. When Laura regained consciousness the laundry room was dark. She had been lying on the cold concrete floor for hours, partially clothed. The party was over and no one heard her anguished sobs.

Laura wrapped a sheet from the laundry basket around her and cautiously made her way to the manager's door. From a brochure she had read at college, Laura knew that the police should be called first.

Although she wanted to accept the manager's offer of a drink of water and a wet washcloth for her bruised and dirty face, she refused both. She also desperately wanted to take a long, hot shower and throw away the clothes she was wearing. The only advice she could recall was that it's best to do nothing until the police arrive, otherwise crucial evidence might be erased. She kept hoping that it was all a bad dream and that she'd wake up at any moment safe in her own bed. The less she participated in her nightmare, the sooner it would be over.

Laura's manager encouraged her to lie down on the couch

and covered her with a blanket. Two police officers arrived within fifteen minutes. Laura was grateful to see that one was a woman.

"I am Sergeant Anderson, and this is Officer Weaver," said the policewoman. "We are here to help you in whatever way we can. Do you want us to take you to the hospital or would you prefer that we call an ambulance?"

"I don't think anything is broken." Lack of sleep along with the stress of the rape made talking an effort for Laura. While Sergeant Anderson continued to question Laura, the other officer left to secure the laundry room for the crime lab, and to search the area for suspects or witnesses.

Laura had never been inside a police car. She sat alone in the back seat separated from the front by a steel grill. There were no handles on the inside back doors. She kept thinking, *How ironic. The real criminal should be sitting here instead of me.* With what little strength she had left, Laura pulled the blanket tightly around her, folding her arms protectively across her heart.

As Laura finished telling me what happened, the nurse came in to set out the evidence collection kit. When she was done, a long row of sterile gloves, plastic envelopes, swabs, slides, and syringes lined the counter. Laura avoided looking at them. I gave her some literature that listed numbers to call for counseling. It also mentioned the emotional and physical symptoms she might experience, and advised her when to come back for additional testing for different forms of venereal disease.

Laura relaxed a little and told me about her job as a computer programmer. But as the doctor entered the room, she became tense, reached for my hand, and held it for most of the next hour.

"Laura, are you ready?" I asked gently.

She looked at me, blinking back tears and fatigue, and whispered "Yes."

The doctor looked weary. He questioned Laura about her

medical history, allergies, surgeries, medications, and sexual past. He asked for details of the rape so that he could look for specific injuries. Laura quickly tired of concentrating and had difficulty responding to some questions.

After the nurse took Laura's pulse, temperature, and blood pressure, the doctor examined her body for general signs of injury, abrasions, and bruises. Samples of her urine, saliva, head hair, pubic hair, fingernail scrapings, and rectal and vaginal swabs were carefully desposited in the packets provided by the police. The doctor sat on a stool with wheels which he rolled back and forth between Laura and the counter holding the accumulating evidence. His white coat had blood smears on it.

Finally the doctor and nurse finished, and Laura breathed deeply for the first time in hours. The nurse gave her some clothing donated by the hospital since her own clothes were needed by the police for further evidence. I made sure she had transportation home. She promised to call the Rape Crisis Center in the next few days to let us know how she was doing.

As I drove home, a pastel sun was pushing back the navy blue night. I suddenly realized that it was February 14—a day when we remember those we care about by giving and receiving tokens of affection.

A day Laura will always remember differently.

Know What To Do

It is important for every woman to be prepared for the possibility of rape. How adequately she responds to the crisis of a sexual attack will be proportionate to how she has been trained to respond. In order of importance, here are the steps.

1. Get to a safe place and contact a family member or a friend you can trust, or call your local rape crisis center for support and information.

2. Call the police.

3. Get medical attention as soon as possible. Unless you need immediate first aid, do not change anything concerning

your appearance. Do not shower, bathe, douche, wash your hands, brush your teeth, comb your hair, eat or drink anything, or use the toilet if at all possible. Don't change or destroy clothing or bedding. Resist the urge to straighten any disorder or clean up any mess.

Women are understandably overwhelmed by the emotional, medical, and legal complications which follow a rape. Lack of information and forethought contribute to the problem. With adequate preparation, decisions aren't as difficult and the trauma of rape is more manageable.

FINDING A SAFE PLACE

The first step, finding a safe place, is not always easy, especially if a woman has never thought of needing an emergency refuge. If she is attacked at home, her first instinct may be to leave. This could put her in further danger as she wanders disoriented through the streets with no destination.

If the assault occurs away from home, it can be harder to find shelter. The victim may be injured or unable to find her way out of an isolated or unfamiliar area. The rapist could still be nearby. He may have taken the woman's purse, clothing, or car.

Like other victims of severe stress, she may act in what might be considered an irrational manner. Some women, unable to cope initially with the trauma of rape, have gone to the store, purchased groceries, and prepared a meal. Others have had their hair cut, teeth cleaned, or car washed as if nothing out-of-the-ordinary had happened. These women may be attempting to show that they are able to deal with stress in a mature manner without falling apart. Some simply do not know how to react.

Most women automatically know what to do if a child swallows a poisonous substance or if their house catches on fire because they have rehearsed the proper procedures over and over in their minds. The immediate chaos caused by a rape can likewise be lessened by formulating a plan before it is needed. One could make arrangements with a neighbor or a friend to have a place available at any hour in case of an attack. If a woman must be in a strange part of town, she should note locations of phone booths and businesses that are open twenty-four hours.

Decide ahead of time who would be most responsive to this kind of call for help. Try to choose someone who is kind, understanding, and enlightened about rape. It does not have to be a family member; it could be a classmate or co-worker. Sometimes a loved one can add to the victim's distress, but a casual friend can remain calm and coherent because of her detachment.

Rape crisis hotlines can provide crisis intervention counseling. These services are usually affiliated with a women's center or a hospital and are funded by government or charitable donations. Rape crisis counselors are primarily concerned citizens who are trained to provide short-term counseling and information on available resources. They also will know the location and availability of any local shelters for rape victims. Help is often there for the family and friends of the survivor as well, to assist them in dealing with their own reactions.

CALLING THE POLICE

After you find a safe place and an advocate, it is important that you make a police report. This will help to catch and convict the rapist, thus preventing him from raping again. The police could also provide protection, moral support, and first aid. They can search for suspects and keep any evidence from being destroyed. They can drive the victim to a hospital where the staff is trained to conduct examinations for evidence.

However, no woman should be forced to report, nor should she feel guilty if she cannot do so. While some women find reporting emotionally satisfying, others see it as a further invasion of their privacy. Notifying the police doesn't obligate anyone to press charges or go through criminal proceedings. A victim can stop the process at any point. An account of the rape can also be given anonymously or through a third party.

It is vital for a woman to know her rights as a citizen and

as a rape survivor so that she is not additionally victimized. She has the right to:

- request that a female officer conduct the initial interview
- have a friend or legal advocate present during questioning
- experience reactions to the rape—hysterics, shock, disorientation, or hostility—without these reactions being considered abnormal
- be treated in a considerate and sensitive manner regardless of the circumstances of the assault
- keep her rape private and out of the news media

Although in the past some victims have been treated callously by policemen, now more women can expect to be dealt with competently by officers trained to handle rape cases. Immediately after an assault, the primary concern of the police should be the victim's well-being, not the investigative process. Only a few basic questions need be asked of her initially. A more detailed report can be made a day or two later.

The ultimate success or failure of a rape investigation is often determined by the first authority figure to talk with the victim. In many instances this person will be a police officer, although it can also be a parent, doctor, pastor, or husband. The rape survivor is affected as much by the attitudes of those who respond as by the aid they offer. If she is blamed, scolded, bullied, or doubted by this person in authority, this not only limits her cooperation with the judicial system but hinders her emotional recovery as well.

GETTING MEDICAL ATTENTION

The third step, medical treatment, is usually a rape survivor's most urgent need. It is advisable for a woman to go to the hospital even if she does not think she is injured. She may be too stressed or shocked by the attack to recognize her injuries, particularly internal ones. Testing for pregnancy and sexually transmitted diseases may also be required. Although most victims don't think about prosecuting the rapist at this time, it is essential to gather medical proof of the violation in case they decide to press charges later.

The right medical evidence can be enough to convict a rapist. This not only includes the presence of seminal fluid, but also documentation of bruises, scratches, and other physical trauma. Even minute bits of evidence such as clothing fibers, strands of hair, or the assailant's skin under the victim's fingernails have been instrumental in linking the attacker to the crime.

The examination for evidence is an uncomfortable procedure to go through at any time, but especially after a rape. Medical personnel need to use discretion and sensitivity to ask the necessary yet embarrassing questions without adding to the patient's distress. Fortitude is needed by the victim to undress and be touched by strangers.

Emergency room attendants have been pressured to humanize their approach in sexual assault cases because hospitals play such a pivotal role in patient recovery. Although they still have low priority over life-and-death emergencies, most women who have been raped no longer have to stay in common waiting rooms, disheveled, dazed, embarrassed, and ignored for hours. Victims should be aware that they have the right to be treated with dignity, privacy, and gentleness by the hospital personnel. Although women have mixed experiences in medical facilities following a sexual attack, many find it comforting to be in a safe, sterile environment surrounded by health care professionals.

Every woman will be better equipped, mentally and emotionally, to handle rape if she remembers these three steps:

1. Get safe.
2. Get help.
3. Get care.

While no one is ever fully prepared for the gruesome reality of rape, when uncertainty is replaced with knowledge, a woman need not be immobilized by an attack. With preparation and practice, she can change the reflex of fear into a reflex of action.

When an emotional injury has taken place, the body begins a process as natural as the healing of a physical wound. Let the process happen.

Colgrove, Bloomfield, and McWilliams

One of the hardest parts of your long-term reactions to rape is impatience with still having reactions at all.

Helen Benedict

4

"What's Happening to Me?"

RECUPERATION

Rape causes a crisis in a woman's life. It makes her feel overwhelmed, powerless, and out of control. All the familiar ways of managing and dealing with the world don't seem to work. In fact, rape will probably be the worst life crisis a woman will ever have to face. All components of a woman's self are violated in a sexual assault. Her property rights are trespassed; perhaps her home or car illegally entered. Her personal possessions are plundered or used as weapons to tie, gag, blindfold, or hurt her. Her physical being is threatened, handled without consent, and usually injured.

"What's Happening to Me?"

Finally the most appalling and intimate violation—her inner self is invaded.

What greater insult can be committed by one human being against another?

NO REACTION IS THE SAME

It's impossible to summarize how individuals react after a sexual assault. Each woman has her own method of dealing with a personal crisis—and her response should not be judged as right or wrong. A recuperation from rape depends on many factors: age and maturity of the victim, personality, upbringing, and overall condition at the time; the specifics of the attack; and the support—or lack of support—received after the experience. Consequently, no two women will react the same.

One additional factor plays a pivotal role in one's recovery—the individual's perception of what has happened to her. Those who are the least prepared and have the most difficulty are those who have trouble believing that rape actually happens and happens without provocation. The victim's perception of the crime is central and crucial because experiences that meet our expectations are easier to handle, even if they are painful and difficult. When we know what to expect, we can adjust more readily to reality.

THE RAPE TRAUMA SYNDROME

Generally a woman will go through three stages after a sexual assault: impact, recoil, and reorganization. These stages are similar to the responses in other life crises such as murder, kidnapping, or war. Many experts on sexual violence classify this recovery process as the "rape trauma syndrome."[1] Others label it as "post traumatic stress disorder" since all victims of severe trauma, including rape, experience the same range of emotions.[2]

Just as we need time to heal from physical wounds, we need to go through these phases of recovery for emotional restoration. However, there is one important difference between physical and emotional wounds: Physical injuries usually heal in a few weeks or months; healing for psychological damage may take years. Victims rarely progress from one stage to the next without frequent relapse or blurring of the boundaries between each step. Assimilating a rape into one's life is a slow and measured process for most people. To assure a complete and healthy recovery, each woman should be allowed to determine her own pace.

Impact. The impact phase begins at the time of the rape or soon afterward. Women usually display one of two styles of reactions. Those with *expressed style* have outbursts of emotions including hysteria, crying, confusion, and agitation. Their sense of personal intactness has been shattered. Decision-making falters and simple problems seem insoluble. They may be physically immobilized or move around aimlessly. Feelings of helplessness, vulnerability, and abandonment are common.

Some women think they're going crazy because they are experiencing so many uncontrollable emotions at one time. When Barbara Blake finally found someone to call the police after frantically knocking on numerous doors, she was near collapse. An ambulance was summoned and she was given oxygen. Barbara said her mind just kept going in circles, she was so overwhelmed by what had happened. For months following the attack, it seemed impossible for her to make simple choices such as what to cook for dinner or what to watch on television.

Other women may react in the *controlled style.* They appear deceptively calm, composed, and subdued. They might even make jokes about what happened. They may have trouble convincing others—and themselves—an attack took place because their's isn't the stereotypic response people often expect.

Women who show this outward tranquility are probably in a state of shock. Their emotional hurt is greater than their ability to cope. Often when we encounter deep psychological pain our minds short-circuit the pain and bury it within our subconscious until we are strong enough to recall it. Because they don't know how to deal with the shock of a sexual attack, some women attempt to stabilize their lives by pretending nothing happened.

49

"What's Happening to Me?"

"For the first week I simply refused to believe I was raped," revealed Ellen Foster. "I continued to tell the police that I was just robbed. I didn't want to burden my parents with the truth. More than anything, I wanted to go on living my life exactly as I had before the rape. I have since learned that my initial shock was a shield, protecting me from intense pain. It wore off gradually until I could bear the hurt without as much protection."

Physical trauma is also a part of the impact phase. Soreness and bruising caused by the attack may be present in various parts of the body such as the arms, legs, breasts, and neck. Some women complain of an irritated throat and difficulty swallowing, especially those who were forced to have oral sex. The ordeal might also have left a woman plagued with headaches, stomach ailments, and burning, itching, or pain in the genitals. Nausea or loss of appetite aggravates her overall ill health because she doesn't feel like eating. Sleeplessness and nightmares may disturb her rest.

Since all emotions are expressed one way or another through our bodies, it is not unusual for a woman to develop other illnesses seemingly unrelated to the assault. The intense feelings of hatred, anger, and bitterness caused by a rape can lower her resistance and activate a variety of diseases. Sometimes sickness can be psychologically induced and used as a plea for attention by a rape victim who feels neglected.

As the initial stress of the attack diminishes, the body's biochemical balance returns to normal. Extensive medical treatment or diagnostic testing is probably not necessary unless symptoms persist. Aspirin, muscle relaxants, or sleeping pills can help relieve temporary discomfort brought on by the crisis as long as the victim follows recommended dosages.

During this first phase—when it is hardest to do so—the victim must think rationally about numerous other matters concerning the attack, such as:

Should I report it to the police?

Do I need medical treatment for a sexually transmitted disease?

How can I pay for doctor's fees or counseling?

What will the reaction of my family and friends be?

Will the rapist approach me again?

Few women can handle all of these crucial questions or decisions—in addition to the rape—without outside support. Unfortunately, in the first reaction stage when she requires it most, a victim is least likely to understand her need for help. Sometimes, especially without outside assistance, a woman may be overwhelmed and suffer a complete breakdown.

In other life crisis situations a person automatically reaches out to others and receives needed support, compassion, and kindness. If there is a death, illness, or accident, people respond with cards, prayers, visits, and meals. In the case of a rape, even if a victim asks for help, many people don't know how to react. Though they may mean well, they often respond in ways that are ineffective and damaging. Helping a woman who has been raped can be frightening because you are reminded of your own vulnerability. This fear makes you want to resolve the situation quickly by saying something terse or curt to the victim. (Chapter 8 gives a list of suggestions on how to help a rape victim.)

This phase is complete when the victim resolves the initial anxiety and returns to a somewhat normal lifestyle. This crisis stage is the shortest since it is a time of extreme upheaval and severe stress. A woman cannot tolerate its intensity for more than a few days or a couple of weeks.

Recoil. In the second phase, the victim appears to have made a satisfactory adjustment. She has tackled the upsetting issues of whether to involve the police and hospital and what to tell people about the assault. She is no longer acutely upset, and convinces others that her life is back to normal. Usually, however, the problem is only suppressed.

During this time a woman must still deal with a number of distressing emotions including guilt, anger, fear, depression, and self-pity. Because these feelings are powerful and painful, they cannot be confronted all at once. Thus, the second stage, aptly called recoil, involves two kinds of activity: denial and

51

resolution. Sometimes the victim will be unable to think about the assault and its aftermath so she ignores what happened; at other times she will be able to feel and work on resolving these enormous conflicts. Then, after she has struggled with the crisis for a while, she becomes tired and again represses her troubles to recuperate for the next confrontation. This process has been compared to the natural cycle of sleeping and waking and has been described as "waxing and waning of tension."[3]

Between these periods of denial, the victim struggles to face some of her inner trauma. Fear is one of the most difficult emotions to confront. She may relive the crime repeatedly in her mind, agonizing over what she could have done differently. Often women who were numb during the assault feel the full intensity of their terror once they are in a safe place—then they realize how close they came to being killed.

"I was more afraid months after the rape than I was during it or immediately afterwards," recalled Barbara Blake. "I was home alone one evening watching the news. They reported that a young girl had been assaulted and murdered in our town. I started imagining how terrified she must have been and related it to my attack. I became so frightened that I started shaking and hyperventilating. I had to call a girlfriend to come over and spend the night with me."

Sometimes, a woman must become emotionally separated from the rape experience for a time so that she can resume her normal activities and reassure those worried about her. In an effort to suppress what has happened, some even neglect safety precautions rather than admit that the incident has affected them. For example, one woman wandered around town late at night all alone. Another went on a fishing trip with a group of men she had just met. Ann Crawford continued to see her psychologist several times after the rape. She tried to rationalize the assault by telling herself, *I wasn't a virgin anyway. He didn't hurt me that bad, it could have been worse. Maybe he thought it was part of my therapy.*

Others use different forms of distractions until they can confront the pain again. Some throw themselves into compulsive activities to avoid any reflection of the incident. A woman may antiseptically clean her home from top to bottom (perhaps subconsciously related to her feelings of uncleanness from the rape). Another diversion can be involvement in numerous community or job-related ventures or completing long-neglected or postponed projects. For some, filling out police forms, contacting various agencies, or following the progress of the criminal investigation of her crime can provide the needed diversion.

Each woman must determine the recuperative rhythm best for her. Only she knows when and for how long she can grapple with the rape's repercussions. Often this selective process revolves around the people and circumstances in her life. Elizabeth Green's cycle fluctuated with the schedules of her three young children. Because they had already been upset by their parents' divorce, she tried to remain as normal as possible in front of them. When they were at school or asleep she would cry or call a friend to vent some of her despair. Ellen Foster often structured her recoiling around difficult symphony performances when she could not afford to have her mind on anything but the music and the conductor.

A woman who has been raped *must* stay in touch with some part of her life which she views as secure, stable, and familiar— otherwise she will lose her grip on reality. When a person is in a severe trauma, they often feel they are outside the realm of normal life. Simple everyday chores such as gardening or cooking can give a sense of still being a part of the real world.

Because the victim appears well-adjusted in front of some people and distraught in front of others, this phase confuses family and friends. The mood swings also discourage the victim, especially if she isn't aware of why she has ups and downs. When depressed, she may easily forget her progress and feel that she'll never recover.

While repressing emotions offers protection, allowing feelings to surface offers resolution; this gives a woman the energy and determination to make whatever changes are necessary to rebuild her life. She may feel the need to move, change her schedule, job, or school to avoid people and places associated with her attack. Adding security measures to her home, taking self-assertiveness training, or recognizing the support of individuals formerly taken for granted can help the survivor of rape regain her confidence.

"While some defense mechanisms are normal responses to stressful situations, their overuse can cause additional problems since they actually distort our perception of reality," warns Dr. G. Keith Olson, psychologist and author of *Counseling Teenagers*. He continues:

> If a woman does not get appropriate support during this second crisis stage, her defenses may come back together in a dysfunctional way that can create psychological disorders later in life.
>
> A broken bone that has been left untended will knit back together by itself, but may then have to be rebroken and reset long after the first break. Women who have been sexually assaulted sometimes reconstruct their defenses in ways that create problems in their future life adjustments. These dysfunctional defense systems will have to be disassembled and rebuilt in the future, probably through extensive therapy.
>
> Ambivalence toward men, low self-esteem, chronic depression, and sexual problems are some indications the initial injury has not properly healed. Many of my clients have been women seeking help for presumably unrelated complaints which were actually caused by never dealing effectively with a rape.[4]

Since each victim and her assault are highly individualized, it is impossible to predict how long one might remain in this second stage of recovery. If the crime occurred prior to or during adolescence, this phase may last years because the victim had to mature before she could deal with her feelings. This was particularly true in Cathy Campbell's life since her first rape at thirteen was compounded by a second, more brutal assault when she was fifteen. Because of her youth and lack of support, she lingered in the middle phase until her late twenties.

Even in the best of circumstances, it is not unusual to be in the recoil period for a year. Tragically, some women never progress out of this stage. They repress the incident for their lifetime, never resolving it. These are usually women who do not have the resources within or outside themselves to successfully integrate the experience into their lives.

Reorganization. During phase three the survivor of rape begins to put the experience into perspective: The crime is no longer the focus of her life. Feelings of anger and fear diminish, giving her emotional energy to invest in other areas. Her mental state becomes more balanced as the need to deny the victimization declines. Although she may still talk about the assault, it will be with greater composure. Some women may never mention it again.

Women in the reorganization stage recognize the world is not as safe as once thought and continue to take steps to ensure their security. A survivor sees how to prevent a future attack, but she no longer blames herself for the previous one. Rather than deciding to mistrust everyone, she carefully selects whom she can trust. There are still black moments, but they are fewer and farther apart. She knows complete recovery may be distant and at times difficult, yet there is hope; the goal is attainable.

Since sexual violence is so prevalent, the woman can be frequently reminded of her own victimization long after it occurred. She may read of a similar attack in the newspaper or be asked to aid another victim. Such reminders can evoke some of the earlier pain echoing the first-stage reactions, but the episode is usually short-lived and muted in comparison.

HELP DURING THE RECUPERATION PROCESS

Without diminishing the seriousness of rape and its potential for physical and psychological damage, one must be careful not to regard rape as "a fate worse than death." A woman should guard against making her assault a lifetime burden.

The time it takes for a woman to go through the three

stages of the rape trauma syndrome is critical because, during that time, psychological forces are set in motion which determine the course of her recovery. Often a survivor of rape is overwhelmed and impatient with the recuperative process. Unlike a physical cure, an emotional healing is imperceptible, and there is nothing more despairing than a deep-seated fear that you are never going to get better.

However, our spirits have natural restorative abilities, as do our bodies. Sometimes all we need to get us on the road to recovery is an adequate understanding of the ailment and the right information to combat its ill effects. Recovery can be delayed or thwarted if there is no effective plan of action to follow. Our position is strengthened when we know that we are heading in the right direction even if we have a long way to go.

The following ten suggestions are given to help alleviate this sense of helplessness and to build the necessary scaffolding to reconstruct your life.

1. *Accept that the rape will change your life; not ultimately make it worse, just different.* Your relationships will be altered, the way you perceive life and how you feel about yourself will never be the same. People often stay in ruts or unhealthy habits because change is frightening. However, change can reveal choices and personal strengths previously unrecognized. In the classical Chinese language, the word for *crisis* and *opportunity* are the same word. It helps to have their perspective.

2. *Structure your days* so you won't be prone to depression. Make a list of things you want to get done and try to do them one by one. Celebrate small successes. Allow each accomplishment to give you a sense of mastery as you regain control of your life. Do not force yourself to take on more than you can comfortably handle, and do not be afraid to say "no" to others' demands.

3. *Take care of yourself physically.* When you are under stress, it's easy to forget the basic ways to reduce stress: eat proper foods, drink plenty of water, take vitamins (particularly B and C), and get moderate exercise. Don't abuse alcohol, drugs, or food, especially sugar and caffeine. Also, remember that the

way you look affects the way you feel, so don't neglect personal grooming.

4. *Change your surroundings.* Different scenery can alter your way of seeing things. Rearrange your furniture, sleep in a different room, drive a new route to the store. Travel if you can, even if it is just a short distance. If you live in an urban area, get out into nature. Take a trip to the city if you live in the country.

5. *Be good to yourself.* Give yourself a present—a bouquet of fresh flowers, a cuddly stuffed animal, a bottle of scented bath oil—that says you care about you. Enjoy tranquility. Take time to watch a sunset. Play music that cheers you, not that reinforces your low mood.

6. *Combat negative thoughts and feelings.* All of us coach or counsel ourselves in ways that are either damaging or useful. Watch how you talk to yourself. Concentrate on what you did right, not wrong. Remind yourself that you survived the rape, that you are now safe, and that your reactions are not bizarre. Don't watch television programs or movies which exploit women or encourage sexual violence. Limit the amount of news which is mostly negative, that you absorb.

7. *Be expressive.* Tears and laughter are excellent stress relievers. Allow yourself to cry, but keep your sense of balance about unanswered questions and unresolved heartache. Our brain has its own pharmacy, and laughter releases a positive chemical reaction to restore you naturally. Some hospitals even have "laugh rooms" because doctors are recognizing the healing value of humor. Pour out your feelings in a journal or diary if you can't express yourself verbally.

8. *Maintain a strong support group.* We are created to be interdependent. Survivors of rape who isolate themselves have a longer and harder time recovering. Be careful about depending on one or two people to meet all your emotional needs. It is better to have a larger base of support. Avoid those who get you down by lecturing, blaming, or minimizing your assault.

9. *Don't be afraid to seek professional help.* You don't have to

be crazy or neurotic to see a therapist or counselor. Asking for help from people trained to deal with victims is a sign of strength and resourcefulness, not weakness. They can assist you in sorting out your problems, reviewing your coping strategies, and gaining insights that will facilitate your recovery. Ask for recommendations from agencies, friends, your pastor, or doctor. It is vital that you find someone who understands the rape trauma syndrome and has experience dealing with survivors of sexual assault.

10. *Give yourself time to heal.* Recovering from rape is a lengthy process for most women. Resist comparing your rate of recovery with someone else's. Just be the best you can be. Value your uniqueness, instead of judging yourself on the basis of other people's standards and perceptions. You are not abnormal; what happened to you was abnormal. Have faith in your own ability to decide what will be the best treatment for you.

PEOPLE DON'T HAVE TO BE VICTIMS

Like other life crises, recovering from rape is a long-term process which often gives the survivor an opportunity to make changes for the better.

Psychologist Ann Kaiser Stearns says in *Living Through Personal Crisis*:

> People don't have to be victims. Whatever the loss, however terrible it was. Our sorrow can be integrated, can teach us something about ourselves and about life, can be claimed as a part of ourselves. Even horrible losses can be transformed into learning. . . . Sometimes the one thing that keeps us going is the knowledge that human beings can find the courage to survive, to transform something terribly hurtful or ugly into positive learning and growing.[5]

While rape itself is never a positive encounter, many women relate experiencing some beneficial results. Some survivors report feeling stronger and gaining an increased awareness of just being alive. They are more sensitive and thoughtful of others. Similar to a person whose terminal illness is arrested, they have examined and altered their values. Others have emerged from the trauma with new goals, aspirations, and ways of coping with other stressful situations.

Barbara Blake said, "Surviving the attack has reminded me how fragile life is and how much we need each other. I'm now not only more considerate of others than I was before the rape, I'm more considerate of myself. I know my limitations, but I also have discovered strengths I never knew I had."

Rape is no different from any other crime of violence. While it is frightening, disgusting, and painful—it is not demeaning. You are the same worthwhile, lovable person you always were. You do not have to become one of rape's marred-for-life victims, because you *choose* your own response. When you are psychologically prepared for rape, you can stay in control and refuse to be destroyed.

1. Ann Wolbert Burgess and Lynda Lytle Holmstrom, *Rape Victims of Crisis* (Bowie, Md.: Robert J. Brady Co., 1974).
2. Judith Rowland, *The Ultimate Violation* (Garden City, N.Y.: Doubleday & Co., 1985), p. 336.
3. Morton Bard and Dawn Sangrey, *The Crime Victim's Book* (New York: Basic Books, 1979), p. 40.
4. G. Keith Olson, *Counseling Teenagers* (Loveland, Colo.: Thom Schultz Publications, 1984). Qoute from an interview with Dr. Olson, April 24, 1987.
5. Ann Kaiser Stearns, *Living Through Personal Crisis* (New York: Random House, 1984), pp. 140-41.

An act of rape, even though it may take only minutes, is so deep a violation that it can shatter the self-worth a woman has taken a lifetime to build.

Linda Tschirhart Sanford

Physical injuries are usually quickly healed with the aid of physicians and modern medical technology. Emotional injuries are stubborn and elusive, taking much time and effort to heal and sometimes defying help altogether.

David B. Peters

5

"Why Is It Taking Me So Long to Get Better?"

———————————————————————————

DISABILITIES

66 **I** pretended to be recovered from my rape long before I actually was," said Elizabeth Green. "Once my bruises were gone, most people thought that I was over it. I was embarrassed for others to know it still bothered me. I even tried to convince myself that I was okay when deep down inside I knew differently."

Rape is more than just physical abuse.

It leaves emotional injuries which linger long after the body is healed. Although there is an illusion of recovery when the physical trauma is repaired, the real trauma, the victim's invisible wounds of mental anguish, often go unnoticed and unattended by others.

Rape crisis counselors often receive calls from women struggling with the emotional pain of an assault which occurred ten or twenty years before. Their physical damage has long since mended, but they have harbored their psychological hurt without knowing how to resolve it. These persistent and disabling emotional injuries fall into five main categories: diminished self-esteem, sexual problems, crippling fears, difficulty trusting people, and predisposition to being victimized again.

LOSS OF SELF-ESTEEM

One of the most devastating consequences of rape is the assault on a woman's sense of self-worth. Rape has the potential of reinforcing all of the negative feelings about oneself, and destroying all the positive ones. A survivor often experiences a significant loss of self-esteem that begins with the attack and may continue for a long time. Many women report feeling permanently soiled, used, ashamed, and worthless. Some victims go to extraordinary, and sometimes harmful, lengths to cleanse themselves by compulsively bathing, douching, or washing their mouths with strong disinfectants. One woman soaked in a bathtub filled with household bleach. Approximately 10 percent of rape victims (as did Ellen Foster and Cathy Campbell) contract a venereal disease from the rapist. This further lowers their feelings of worth.

"The most frightening thing after my rape was that I didn't know if I would ever become myself again," said Ellen. "I felt I had become another person. I liked myself before. I didn't like who I had become. Before the rape I was usually relaxed, stable, and capable of accepting challenges and handling pressure. Afterwards I was tense, unpredictable, and frustrated with simple decisions like which pair of shoes to wear. I was angry at the rapist who had taken away the real me. That man did the worst possible thing—in violating my body he stripped me of my being."

It is common for a woman to blame herself for the attack

because of the prevailing myths surrounding sexual violence and the insinuating comments from others. Often she feels that her physical appearance caused the rape. She may then try to disguise her sexuality by wearing baggy clothing, cutting her hair short, or gaining or losing weight. If she was wearing something revealing at the time of the assault, such as a night-gown or a bathing suit, her self-incrimination is likely to be worse.

According to Lynette Marie Galisewski, a licensed therapist, "The misconception that a woman is somehow re-sponsible for being raped is terribly destructive for the victim. It not only makes other people blame a woman for the rape, it makes her blame herself. Many of my clients have developed a tremendous self-hatred for the way they look, walk, dress, and behave, as if one or more of these were responsible for their getting raped. Their guilt is so intense that some attempt to kill themselves."

A woman may be forced to make major changes which further undermine her sense of well-being. If the assault oc-curred in her home or neighborhood, she may no longer feel safe and may have to move from a favored residence. Ellen lived alone for years and valued her independence. After the rape, she was afraid to be by herself so she sold her home and went to live with her parents.

Other victims have had to leave school just before gradu-ation because they were unable to concentrate on finals. Some have quit a promising career because of the disruption caused by the assault. Ellen feared that she would be replaced as principal percussionist since she now had difficulty performing in public concerts. Some women become alienated from their families if their rape is doubted or if the offender was a relative. Others have been pressured to leave churches when the rapist was someone in the congregation and no one believed it.

The subject of rape makes people uncomfortable. Nearly everyone is embarrassed for the victim. She senses this and often doesn't have the energy or motivation to find the people who can handle the discomfort. Many women feel as if the word *raped* is stamped on their foreheads and they have difficulty approaching others. A victim may project her own feelings of repulsion onto others and shy away from human support at the time she needs it most. In addition, her seemingly irrational behavior and accompanying low self-esteem can drive away the most faithful supporter.

For several reasons, the self-esteem of Christian women is shattered even worse than the self-esteem of non-Christian women by rape. First, according to Dr. James Dobson, low self-esteem is already the most troubling problem for women in the church.[1] Secondly, many Christians believe that they are exempt from misfortune if they live "right," so if a woman is raped, it was either her fault or God's punishment for sin. Thirdly, since the church is not open or informed about sexual violence, the Christian victim must turn to secular resources for help. This may add further to her guilt and low self-worth if she feels that rape is the unmentionable sin.

A survivor of rape often struggles alone to regain her sense of self-worth. She must learn to reject negative labels from other people, even those whose opinions she values. She needs to stop condemning herself for being in the wrong place at the wrong time. Blaming the rapist and not herself is an important step in rebuilding her esteem. Making new friends, perhaps other rape victims, joining interesting organizations, and engaging in positive activities can all help restore self-respect.

Finally, the survivor needs to recognize that despite how she and others perceive her, she has deep significance and great worth as a creation of God. His love is personal and specific, sustaining us, transforming our weaknesses, conquering our liabilities. God's love is the most important influence on our sense of well-being.

FEELINGS ABOUT SEX ARE AFFECTED

Considering the nature of rape, it is not surprising that it has a significant impact on one's feelings about sex. After an assault, sexual problems range from frigidity to promiscuity with a wide range in between. Some women totally withdraw from men, unable to tolerate any physical intimacy. Others develop relatively normal relationships, marry, but have difficulty fully enjoying sex. Many become promiscuous, unable to achieve permanence or fidelity in sexual relations.[2] When a woman associates sex with the pain and terror of the rape instead of pleasure and security, she may have considerable trouble forming and sustaining sexual bonds.

The rape survivor will probably be afraid and uncomfortable with even the thought of sex for a number of months after the assault. It will take time and patience to rebuild the trust and intimacy which the rapist damaged. Years later, some victims still encounter occasional feelings of panic and disgust during lovemaking.

A rape can be especially damaging for a virgin. It is devastating to be initiated into sex in such a degrading and brutal manner. The assault can leave lasting psychological trauma, more so when the woman and others believe what happened to her was an act of sex, not violence. She may not realize the difference between normal sexual relations and rape, fearing that they are similar. If she was taught to value her virginity and that men will marry only virgins, she must not only deal with the crisis of the attack but her entire future as well.

It is vital that both sex partners realize the difference between sexual activity and sexual violence. The rape was an act of violence, not an act of sex. When the two are equated or confused, the married woman may see her victimization as adultery and feel that she has been unfaithful to her husband. Others may also see the rape as infidelity, especially if the victim knew her assailant. This was true with Ann Crawford's and Elizabeth Green's rapes: Many believed that they had been involved in extramarital affairs.

The sexual perversions that often accompany rape add further turmoil. Since a high percentage of rapists are either impotent or unable to ejaculate, a sexual assault frequently consists of a woman being violated orally, anally, or with a foreign object. The wife and the husband may have difficulty resolving the feeling that she participated in perverted sex acts against their moral standards. Still more difficulty comes in resolving the issues of a rare, but possible pregnancy, or more

65

commonly, a sexually transmitted disease resulting from a rape. Many victims are now understandably concerned that the rapist had AIDS and that they may unknowingly infect their husbands.

Sex is a delicate topic between most couples at the best of times. When sex has been violated by rape, the subject is even harder to discuss. Yet men and women need to tell each other what they are thinking and feeling in order to resolve sexual difficulties. The wife may think her husband is avoiding sexual contact because he finds her soiled, when he is actually being sensitive about resuming relations too soon. The husband may feel rejected when, in reality, the woman is just not ready for sexual intimacy. If these thoughts are not communicated, it can further compound the couple's problems.

It is usually more productive to focus on nonsexual ways of renewing intimacy rather than rushing sex or pretending that the rape did not change anything. Physical affection without sexual expectations can bring a couple closer together when one or both is not ready to resume relations. A meal at a favorite restaurant, a social event they both enjoy, or learning to pray together can all help strengthen a marriage that is shattered by rape.

No matter how stable a relationship, most couples go through a difficult time after a rape. Various studies show a 40-90 percent breakup rate between couples after a rape, although some experts say most of these marriages were already weak.[3] Trauma or anxiety of any kind is likely to affect sexuality, yet rape doesn't have to destroy a marriage. Some people are brought closer together by this tragedy. It's worth seeking counseling if the couple's sexual problems seem insurmountable. With time and understanding a good sexual relationship can usually be restored.

CRIPPLING FEARS

Every recovering survivor of rape deals with a number of fears associated with the attack. One of the most common is the fear of death. While rapists who kill their victims are relatively rare, most use the threat of death, accompanied by verbal or physical abuse, to gain a woman's cooperation. Like other crimes of violence, rape leaves the victim with the feeling that "I could have been killed." This realization of being suddenly thrust into a life-threatening situation can add a great deal of fear and confusion to one's life. On the other extreme, there can be feelings of elation at having lived through the attack.

Many fears are related to the rapist and the circumstances of the assault. It's normal to dread seeing the rapist again or to be afraid he may attack another time. Phobias of men who are the same age, occupation, race, or physical appearance as the offender are common. If the victim was alone when she was assaulted, she may now fear being by herself. If she was molested in a public place, she may then fear leaving her home or being around people.

Surroundings, smells, or sounds reminiscent of the attack can suddenly evoke feelings of terror. After her rape Ellen Foster never wanted to be the first one to enter a dark room. Even though she'd received an unlisted number, she panicked when the phone rang since the rapist had made obscene calls to her before breaking into her home. Something as innocent as electrical duct tape became a painful reminder because Ellen was bound with it during her assault.

Anniversary dates are usually thought of as celebrations in our culture, but we forget that traumatic events also have an anniversary. For a number of years, the anniversary of a rape can stir up emotions the victim thought were resolved. Depending on when the rape happened, certain seasons of the year or weather conditions can renew fears associated with the attack. Ironically, Barbara Blake was attacked while her city commemorated Crime Prevention Week. Ellen Foster's rape occurred just prior to Easter, her favorite and busiest time as a musician.

Many times a woman will fear telling others about the rape for a number of reasons. She may be afraid that people will view her as a disgrace, as stupid, or as someone to be pitied. She's embarrassed to discuss it, especially when people seem overly curious about the details. Many women hesitate to tell anyone because they don't want to be the subject of gossip or rumors.

While telling others certainly doesn't guarantee a positive, helpful response, not telling anyone prevents a victim from receiving any possible assistance or support. Rape, like other tragedies of life, is easier to bear if the victim can find at least one person in whom she can confide.

The survivor won't feel as if she's going crazy if she remembers that her fears are normal and will lessen in intensity. After a woman's anxieties have diminished somewhat, she needs to confront and deal with them. It might help if she makes a list of her fears and tries to face the smallest ones first. If she represses her fears over the years, they can become permanent disabilities, doing more damage than the rape warranted.

Those helping the victim need to realize that her phobias may cause her to act irrationally from time to time. If a woman can admit her fears and explain why she is afraid, it will help others to be more supportive. Joining a survivor's support group is often beneficial as the members can help each other resolve their common fears.

DIFFICULTY TRUSTING

A rape usually erases some of the security and trust a woman has in the world and those around her. This loss of trust particularly affects her relationships with men.

Most women grew up believing that males are the people in authority. A husband, a father, a pastor, or a boss is often the controlling influence in a woman's life. When a rapist takes that same control and uses it to hurt and humiliate her, a woman may be afraid to relinquish control to any man in the future.

The victim's trust is sometimes further eroded by those who come to her aid after an assault. Most police officers, doctors, lawyers, and judges are men. They often have the power either to reinforce the survivor's wariness or to help her regain the trust she lost, depending on how they treat her.

A husband, boyfriend, brother, or father can make the woman withdraw further because his reaction is often angry. He's angry at the rapist and wants retaliation. He's angry at himself for not being able to prevent the rape. He may be angry at the victim for being too weak to defend herself or for being careless. He's angry at the police for not catching the rapist. But a victim doesn't need to see any more anger, she's already been the target of one man's rage.

How a woman reacts is partly dependent on her prior involvements with men. If her relationship with her father, husband, or other important men in her emotional development was detrimental, she will have a harder time trusting men again. Elizabeth Green was in an abusive marriage when she was assaulted by her neighbor. When Cathy Campbell's father died shortly after she was raped by a policeman, she was doubly devastated. Both women's mistrust of male authority became deeply imbedded. Cathy, especially, showed her disregard for parental and legal control by her numerous scrapes with the law.

If the rape was nonviolent and the rapist was known to the victim, people may think that she would have an easier time adjusting than if she were brutally attacked by a stranger. The opposite is closer to the truth. When the rape is more like "normal sex," it is harder for the woman and others to distinguish between sexual violence and sexual activity. Many will have a hard time believing that it was really rape. When the assailant was someone a woman trusted, she may doubt her ability to accurately judge a man's character. After a rape by a stranger, a woman mistrusts strangers. After a rape by an acquaintance, she may mistrust everyone.

Other circumstances can also erode a woman's trust in people. Sometimes those in whom she has confided will violate her faith in them by telling others of the rape without her permission. Some may make insensitive comments or disbelieve her story. A few will not be able to handle hearing of the assault at all. Ann Crawford's mother was unwilling to discuss her daughter's rape until years later.

Often, a survivor's relationship with God also needs readjustment. God is usually portrayed as a male in absolute control and Christians are urged to surrender control of their lives to God. This concept can be frightening to a woman who has just had all control taken from her. She needs to be patient with the recovery process and realize that her feelings are to be expected, and that her trust in God can be restored with time.

Everybody needs a certain amount of trust to live securely in the world. It's hard to go through life fearing much of the human race. A woman may avoid the hurtful, but she also avoids the harmless and the helpful. Although it might not seem like it for a while, there are people, including men, whom the survivor can find trustworthy. She will want to be cautious and selective, but in time she needs to be vulnerable to someone. Most people will be worthy of her trust.

VICTIMIZED AGAIN

It's easy for the survivor of a sexual assault to fall into the pattern of being repeatedly victimized. Her self-esteem is low, her life is disoriented, and she may have few, if any, supporters. When she feels that nearly everyone treats her as less than human, she also begins to see herself as worthless.

The rape victim, consciously or subconsciously, often sets herself up for further victimization. Bereaved of positive input from others, she accepts the role of victim. When she considers herself to be "damaged goods," her behavior begins to reinforce her self-hatred. This damaged goods syndrome is expressed in numerous hazardous forms: sexual promiscuity, substance abuse, criminal activity, eating disorders, and violence. Rape victims also have a higher probability of vocational difficulties, divorce, psychological addictions, and suicide.

Prostitution is another common means of reinforcing victimization. Several studies of prostitutes have shown that rape was the first sexual experience for more than two-thirds of them.[4] Prostitution depersonalizes sex into a service, not a relationship. It tends to devalue both people involved and further demoralizes the woman by alienating her from most of society.

Religious beliefs sometimes make a woman more vulnerable to further victimization. Teachings of the church may prevent a woman from taking self-protection seriously when they mistakenly convince her that God does not allow "good Christians" to be harmed. Women are also taught to be kind to everyone, to help those in need, and that violence is never acceptable.

Biblical instruction was never intended to encourage the victimization of anyone. There are situations where a rude and aggressive response is required to protect oneself. Gentle and kind words are seldom effective with a rapist.

Despite Scripture to the contrary, many Christians still believe that we have to be deserving of God's love and provision. Because a rape victim often doesn't feel worthy of any good, it's difficult for her to understand God's unconditional acceptance. She may even seek punishment from God and others to reinforce her negative self-concept.

OTHERS ARE NEEDED TO SPEED RECOVERY

Comprehensive medical and psychological care should be available for every victim of sexual assault. Almost without exception, professional assistance would hasten the healing process. Without skillful support, rape victims often flounder as Cathy Campbell did: In the years after her attack, she acted out nearly every pattern of victimization mentioned. This contributed to her being raped a second and third time. Cathy said, "I didn't value my life very much after the first rape and my father's death. I set myself up to be used and abused over and over because I really didn't think that I deserved better. Recovery was so difficult when I didn't feel that I was worth saving. Someone finally convinced me that, in God's eyes, I had redeeming value."

Mental pain, as well as physical pain, alerts us to the fact that there is a failure in our body's system requiring attention. If we attempt to ignore the pain, permanent damage or even death can result. Unlike psychic wounds, physical injuries usually have an apparent cause and effect. A person can see bruises, bleeding, and broken bones and know how the injury happened. Mental trauma is rarely as traceable or treatable. Often, an outsider—particularly a professional who understands

71

the repercussions of rape—is needed to help a woman recognize behavioral dysfunctions before they become permanent disorders. This downward spiral is nearly impossible to stop without help. A survivor of rape needs someone who can lovingly challenge her wrong choices.

Women who decide to prosecute the rapist should look at themselves as trail blazers. Five years ago the case would not have gone to court; ten years ago no one would have listened at all.

Dorothy Hicks

In our society, prosecuting a rapist is an act of courage. A woman who will do it is to be admired. But a woman who will not do it shouldn't be regarded with contempt.

Andra Medea and Kathleen Thompson

6

"Is Prosecuting Worth It?"

RELAPSE

Whenever I accompany a rape victim to her court appearance, I sit on the defense's side directly behind the defendant. This is so the victim on the stand can focus on me and avoid looking at her assailant. Her other supporters sit across the aisle on the prosecution side. During the proceedings, they frequently glare at the man accused of rape. We all relive the crime through the victim's own testimony excruciatingly extracted by the defense attorney's intimate questioning. Of all the areas of sexual violence that I am involved with—the writing, the crisis counseling, the hospital accompaniment, and the community education—playing courtroom advocate is the most difficult.

It can also be the most rewarding.

UNDERSTANDING THE STEPS INVOLVED

Prosecuting a rapist can be a frightening and frustrating experience for the victim and her supporters. The legal process is intimidating and burdensome, even for the most competent individual. For some women, the conviction of a rapist is not worth the means used to achieve it. Others feel that the benefits of prosecution outweigh the liabilities.

The success of a rape trial depends primarily on two things: how well prepared the rape survivor is in dealing with the court system, and how convincing her case appears. The first is the most important. The best cases can be lost if a woman is not aware in advance of the countless frustrations, delays, and complications in legal matters. The more one knows about her legal rights and responsibilities as a crime victim, the better her chances for conviction of the rapist.

It is important for a woman to understand all the steps in bringing charges against a rapist. Rape cases are handled differently from state to state and even county to county. Since no two geographic areas are exactly alike in their legal terminology, criminal processing, or sentencing practices, she should seek information from her local police department, district attorney, and rape crisis center before prosecuting. She will have a much better chance of meeting her adversary on equal ground if she is prepared for the confrontation. If a victim is not sufficiently informed before she goes to court, her ability to testify may be impaired or she may give up altogether and lose the case by default.[1]

A convincing rape case depends on a number of factors. Decisions of the judge and jury are often based on their perceptions of the victim and the accused. An acquittal or conviction usually hinges on stereotypical beliefs about which rape stories are believable and which ones are fabricated, what type of woman gets raped, and what type of man rapes.

A woman is more likely to be believed if she is married, over thirty, white, and without any careless or nonconformist behavior. This behavior, which some view as precipitating a rape, may include meeting the rapist in a bar, walking outside alone at night, accepting a ride from a stranger, being involved with drugs, or any sexual activity outside of marriage. Juries are also less likely to believe minority and low-income women or those who knew their assailant before the attack.

The rapist has a greater possibility of conviction if he is single, under twenty-five, a different race than the victim, and has a criminal record. Defendants without a job or a steady girlfriend have been thought guilty much more frequently than an employed married man. Even with overwhelming evidence it is hard to predict how a jury will vote if the accused does not "look like a rapist." The "Voss Road Rapist" of Houston, Texas is serving a prison sentence for four counts of burglary even though he is a suspect in fifty to seventy rapes. Both sides doubted that jurors would convict the good-looking, personable, upper-middle-class man of rape.[2]

When all the complicated legal language is removed, a rape trial must settle the question of who is telling the truth—the victim or the defendant? Or more accurately, who does the jury or the judge choose to believe? While sorting out her word against his, the law concerns itself with at least four major controversial issues which are a part of most rape cases: consent, corroboration, victim's background, and defendant's criminal record. Over the years victims have fared disastrously when challenged by these four legalities.

DID SHE CONSENT?

Nearly all states require the victim to prove she didn't consent to the sexual encounter regardless of the circumstances, even when a stranger breaks into a woman's home and beats her before raping her. This concept is unique to the prosecution of rape: No other victim of crime is questioned about whether they consented to the offense. The very idea is ludicrous. Since the law and the public in general still envision rape as a sexual crime, not a physical assault, the focus is often on the behavior and reputation of the victim, not the assailant.

In 1984, Illinois enacted a law that places the burden of proof on the defendant, not the victim. This "affirmative defense" legislation requires the accused to show that the woman agreed to the liaison.[3] Until other states adopt similar measures, the victim must take the stand to refute the defendant's claims that the act took place without force or threat.

Because both the victim and defendant are entitled to an unbiased jury, any person who has a knowledge of sexual violence, especially if that person has been a victim, is generally excused from jury duty in rape cases. The prosecution is then left with jurors who have never been exposed to sexual assault except through television, films, the news media, and fiction. That juror, therefore, may expect a description of a violent fight between a woman and a stranger with a lethal weapon. And he is suspicious when he discovers that the alleged rapist was the victim's neighbor whom she let into her home.

In the most successful defenses, the rapist has admitted the act took place but the victim agreed to it without coercion. This defense is easy to sell to a naive juror, especially if the rapist seems like a "nice guy." Elizabeth Green's jury had trouble believing she could live next door to a man and not realize he was a rapist. His light sentence suggested that they believed his consent defense even though photographs of Elizabeth's bruised and bloodied body were introduced as evidence.

Some jurisdictions, particularly California, require a cautionary statement read to juries. Judith Rowland, a former San Diego prosecutor, explains the effect of this jury instruction: "If a doubt is raised in the minds of the jurors (it only takes one to hang it) that the defendant thought, although mistakenly, he had consent, a jury must acquit him. Granted, his belief and the doubt raised must be reasonable ones by certain legal standards. But this requires a victim to *prove* lack of consent beyond a reasonable doubt in the face of overwhelming stereotypes and myths surrounding her behavior, while leaving the defendant to merely *raise* a reasonable mistaken doubt."[4]

Historically, women have had to convince a jury that they fought hard to save their bodies and their lives. Without that assurance, a rapist can be acquitted because he mistakenly believed her lack of resistance equaled consent. Victims of rape continue to suffer from society's distrust of their accusations; some women are still asked to take a lie detector test to determine if they are telling the truth. Even now, too many people erroneously believe that a woman can only be raped if she wants to be.

Does Someone Corroborate the Story?

Corroboration is any testimony or evidence provided by someone other than the victim of a crime. Although many states have repealed this requirement in recent years, it is still often needed to get a rape conviction. While a rape victim doesn't have to sustain injuries to win her case, admittedly it helps. Her testimony alone is not sufficient to go to trial—although it is in every other violent crime. In a judicial system that favors the defendant, juries will have difficulty with an rape case that is not corroborated.

Corroborative evidence in a rape trial may include physical injuries; torn or stained clothing; medical evidence of sexual contact; emotional state of the victim; statements of the police, friends, or relatives of the woman. The problem is that frequently there is no corroborative evidence. Many women submit to the rapist rather than risk injury or death. They may unknowingly destroy valuable evidence by bathing, washing, or throwing away stained clothes or linens. Research shows that half of all rapists do not ejaculate[5] or they rape with a foreign object, so there would be less proof of intercourse. A victim may also be too embarrassed, afraid, or ignorant to get medical aid or police assistance. For days, temporary shock might prevent her from telling anyone of the assault.

The juror, without an accurate understanding of rape and the trauma it causes, finds it hard to comprehend the victim's state of mind and behavior. Add to that a lack of corroborative evidence, and most juries can be convinced by a consent defense even under circumstances which are obviously non-consensual.

WHAT IS THE VICTIM'S BACKGROUND?

Courts vary as to whether they will allow evidence of the victim's private life and sexual history to be admitted in a sex crime trial. Whether it is communicated explicitly or implicitly, some jurisdictions still operate on the dubious assumption that an unchaste woman is more likely to lie or to deserve to be raped than is a chaste woman. It is not unusual for defense attorneys to hound rape victims with questions concerning when they lost their virginity and whether they have had intercourse with anyone outside of marriage.

After Ellen Foster's rape, she struggled to a neighbor's house with her face, hands, and feet secured with duct tape. She was disarrayed and confused. Clearly she had been beaten and sexually assaulted. Yet Ellen was still questioned by the authorities about her sexual history and other irrelevant matters, such as the security of her home.

In 1974, Michigan was the first to pass what is still one of the most stringent shield laws: It keeps much of a victim's sexual history confidential. Other progressive states followed Michigan by allowing evidence of prior sexual activity only in limited circumstances, usually when related to previous acts of intercourse between the victim and the defendant.

Legal reformists and victims feel that a woman's sexual history has nothing to do with being raped. That particular line of questioning reflects prejudice, especially when the court fails to examine the defendant's prior sexual acts. At times the defense will ask such questions even when certain of an overruling, in an attempt to plant suspicion against the victim.

Many states have laws designed to protect rape victims from having to reveal details of their private lives. But invariably, a particular clause may allow such testimony if the defense can prove it is relevant. Other factors can then be introduced to cast doubt on the woman's credibility and character.

In the nationally publicized rape that occurred in a bar in New Bedford, Massachusetts in 1983, defense lawyers emphasized the victim's drinking habits, her receipt of welfare, her single parenthood, and her time spent in counseling. The questions related to these factors were designed to focus on the victim's morality and to distract from the behavior of the accused. They also served to divert the jury from the basic question: Did a group of men hold a woman down on a pool table, in front of a number of witnesses, and force her to engage in sexual intercourse with two or more men?[6]

DEFENDANT'S CRIMINAL RECORD OFTEN DISALLOWED

Another ruling favoring the alleged rapist commonly disallows testimony of his previous sex crimes. Data shows that a rapist repeatedly commits the same crime in the same general locality and with the same method of operation. Surely it is relevant, therefore, that the jury know if other women have brought similar charges against the defendant or if he has prior convictions for rape.

Some states have recognized this injustice and have passed a "similar acts" statute, whereby evidence of former offenses is admissible to show a distinctive plan, motive, or identity. The decision to use prior evidence, however, may work in the defendant's favor: Appellate courts often reverse convictions that they declare were obtained primarily by association with a previous criminal act rather than the charged offense.[7]

The defendant has the constitutional right to remain silent and not incriminate himself. Conviction rates are invariably higher when the defendant allows himself to be cross-examined. The burden of proof lies on the prosecution; the defense does not have to present any evidence or call any witnesses. The accused can choose not to testify, while the victim must take the stand and tell a roomful of strangers the details of the rape and other personal matters.

THE BENEFITS OF PROSECUTING

Despite these and other drawbacks of a rape trial, there are some benefits to prosecuting. *It can offer the victim a constructive outlet to ventilate her anger and pain.* Research has shown that women who prosecute often recover from the trauma of rape sooner than those who don't. There is satisfaction in knowing that one has done all that can be done in stopping the rapist from harming someone else.

Experts are convinced that as more men are prosecuted for rape, fewer rapes will be committed. When there is no certainty or severity of punishment, men feel free to rape. Ellen Foster's rapist admitted that while in prison he has researched the various states' penalties for rape so if he is released on parole in 1998 he can live in an area with the shortest sentence.

An alternative to criminal prosecution is to sue the assailant in civil court for damages. Unlike a criminal trial, a civil trial forces the defendant to testify, since in civil court he is not protected by the Fifth Amendment. While most criminals do not have any assets that can be attached, the emotional rewards for a victim can make suing the rapist worthwhile.

A civil suit can also be brought against a business or a third party whose negligence contributed to the crime, even if the rapist has not been caught. A case in point is the civil suit that singer Connie Francis successfully brought against the Howard Johnson Motor Lodge in Westbury, New York in 1976. Miss Francis received nearly $1.5 million in damages from the motel. Her suit charged that inadequate room door locks provided by the motel resulted in her being raped.[8]

A woman may also be eligible for Victims of Violent Crime Compensation. Many states have victim assistance programs to help obtain reimbursement for medical services and counseling costs. The National Organization for Victims' Assistance (NOVA) can provide information about local services or answer questions about prosecution.[9]

LAWS *ARE* CHANGING TO BENEFIT THE VICTIM

For centuries the criminal justice system has been more concerned with the rights of the defendant, especially in rape cases, than the plight of the victim. The rape victim has been guilty until proven innocent. While overall the process may favor the accused, laws are changing these days in behalf of the victim. There are more enlightened men and women involved in the law and on the bench. Nearly every state has passed some form of rape reform legislation. The legal view of rape has slowly evolved from a violent expression of sex to a sexual expression of violence.[10] Pressure from victim's rights groups have resulted in more convictions and greater respect for women who have endured rape. Initially the legal system may seem overwhelming and threatening to a rape victim when she is least prepared to face it. However, if she learns the procedures and pitfalls, and has a great deal of determination, the judicial process is manageable and justice is possible.

1. Morton Bard and Dawn Sangrey, *The Crime Victim's Book* (New York: Basic Books, 1979), p. 126.
2. Robert Draper, "The Gentleman Rapist," *Mademoiselle,*August, 1968, p. 232.
3. Aric Press et al., "Rape and the Law," *Newsweek,* May 20, 1985, p. 60.
4. Judith Rowland, *The Ultimate Violation* (Garden City, New York: Doubleday & Co., 1985), p. 214.
5. Joy Satterwhite Eyman, *How to Convict a Rapist* (Briarcliff Manor, New York: Stein & Day, 1982), p. 84.
6. Six men were brought to trial in the New Bedford rape. Two were acquitted. Of the four men who were convicted, one received a prison sentence of six to eight years and is currently eligible for parole after serving two-thirds of his sentence. The other three are eligible for parole in 1990 after serving two-thirds of a nine- to twelve-year prison term. All four defendants have filed appeals with the Massachusetts Supreme Court for injustices they feel were committed during their trials.
7. Rowland, p. 129.
8. Eyman, p. 62.
9. National Organization for Victim Assistance, 1757 Park Rd. N.W., Washington, DC 20010, (202)232-8560.
10. Kay Marshall Strom, *Helping Women in Crisis* (Grand Rapids, Mich.: Zondervan Publishing House, 1986), p. 102.

The only way to heal the pain that will not heal itself is to forgive the person who hurt you. Forgiving stops the reruns of pain.

Lewis B. Smedes

I am reminded that I have not only survived one of the most hideous, devastating blows to a human being, but through God's grace, I have been able to triumph over it.

Deborah Roberts

7

"Where Is God in All of This?"

RECOVERY

For three months Ann Crawford told no one that her psychologist had raped her. Feeling guilty, stupid, and ashamed, she was simply unable to express her despair to anyone. In her desperate, confused state, she attempted suicide hoping that someone would figure out what was wrong with her. Fortunately, the three half-empty bottles of prescription pills were not lethal. The combination only made Ann extremely ill and she had to be hospitalized.

Ann was raised in the church and was active in Christian

organizations throughout her adolescence. After attending Bible college, she married a seminary graduate and they planted a church on the West Coast. Until the rape, God was always a source of comfort. Now she didn't even want to talk to him. She felt soiled and beyond cleansing, physically and spiritually.

After years of wandering in her own desert, Ann found the help she needed, and she recovered. The following eight steps are part of what Ann discovered during her painstaking pilgrimage. Whether you or someone you know has been raped recently or twenty years ago, these steps are vital for total recovery.

1. Accept that Christians are not immune from the misfortunes of life—including sexual violence. Rape, along with life's other tragedies, can happen to any woman. The providence of God does not always spare Christians from life's adversities. Suffering is a universal experience borne by both the godly and the wicked. The Bible doesn't say that nothing bad will ever happen to us. But it does say in Romans 8:35-39 that nothing that does happen to us can ever separate us from the love of God:

> Who shall separate us from the love of Christ? Shall trouble or hardship or persecution or famine or nakedness or danger or sword? As it is written:
>
> > "For your sake we face death all day long;
> > we are considered as sheep to be slaughtered."
>
> No, in all these things we are more than conquerors through him who loved us. For I am convinced that neither death nor life, neither angels nor demons, neither the present nor the future, nor any powers, neither height nor depth, nor anything else in all creation, will be able to separate us from the love of God that is in Christ Jesus our Lord.

Like many Christian women, Ann assumed she had divine protection from sexual assault. Because she'd never heard rape mentioned in a Christian context, she surmised that it only happened to unbelievers or possibly to backsliders. After her rape she was totally confused. Was she really a Christian? Was God punishing her for some hidden transgression? Ann started investigating other religions and cults because she was no longer sure of the beliefs she had held for years.

Many people view rape as a punishment for sin or as a natural consequence of a victim's wrongdoing. Women have been blamed for their victimization for reasons including: dyeing their hair, failing a biology class, not attending church Sunday nights, and driving the wrong kind of car. People have difficulty believing that painful experiences such as rape happen without provocation, so they create a reason or a higher purpose for their own peace of mind.

Christians search harder for religious answers to the ageless question of why there is suffering. The most frequent explanation is that affliction is God's way of strengthening our character or testing our faith. This implies that God planned a woman's rape—*which is never the case*. Blaming either the victim or God for a sexual assault is a superstitious and simplistic response which avoids placing responsibility where it rightly belongs—on the rapist.

Why are women raped? The most credible answer is that Satan is the instigator. An innocent person reaps the consequences of someone else's sinful choice. God allows such sinfulness because he has given every person a free will and he doesn't stop people from choosing unrighteous acts. The Bible teaches us that evil is always at war with good. God has warned in 1 Peter 5:8 that "your enemy the devil prowls around like a roaring lion looking for someone to devour."

2. Incorporate your Christianity with your assault. Since rape is often a taboo discussion in the Christian community and few women have heard their pastors mention it from the pulpit, they may conclude that it is not a subject to talk about with God. The attack may have been so repulsive and embarrassing that the victim never voices the incident to anyone, including God. The chasm becomes deeper when, as in Ann's situation, the offender was someone she thought she could trust. Her faith in God is understandably shaken.

"Where is God in All of This?"

Abandoning your spiritual life until you get your problem solved only compounds the problem. Many women erroneously believe that the rape has made them sinful or unspiritual, and they don't feel worthy of God's love. The spirituality of a rape victim must be brought into her whole experience; this is her only hope for restoration.

A Christian victim must overcome an additional obstacle: many people stifle the efforts of an individual believer to express any negative thoughts or feelings. This is particularly damaging to a survivor of rape. Not many understand how she truly feels. They discount the seriousness of her assault. She may be urged to praise God when she feels abandoned by him. She may be offered Bible verses and platitudes which sound cruel and superficial to her. She may be pressured to carry on as if everything is normal when, in fact, her world has fallen apart.

It's difficult to recover when no one validates your painful feelings. All wounds need a nurturing environment in which to heal. It is hard to feel God's comfort when you're not supported by those closest to you. It's not easy to integrate your Christian faith with your rape when you doubt God understands, when you feel he's responsible for your distress, and when you fear further estrangement if you pray these feelings of despair. That's why Ann concluded suicide was her only option.

At such times it's better to keep praying honest prayers than to cut off all communication with God just because you don't have anything positive to say. Biblical accounts of the lives of God's most faithful servants include similar laments. David says in Psalm 13:1-2, "How long, LORD? Will you forget me forever? How long will you hide your face from me? How long must I wrestle with my thoughts and every day have sorrow in my heart? How long will my enemy triumph over me?" and in Job 3:25-26, Job cries, "What I feared has come upon me; what I dreaded has happened to me. I have no peace, no quietness; I have no rest, but only turmoil." Jesus himself knew what it was like to feel frightened and alone when he prayed from the cross, "My God my God, why hast thou forsaken me?"

No matter how severe the sexual assault or your despair in dealing with it, never think that you suffer alone or that God has turned away. He's always merciful, sympathetic, and loving toward you. He has promised never to leave or forsake us, even when our senses scream the opposite: "Never will I leave you, never will I forsake you" (Hebrews 13:5).

3. Remember that you are wounded, not dead. And for every wound there is a healing process. Many women think they'll never recover from rape. While it's natural to feel that way, it is another means Satan uses to further destroy a victim's life. When you consider your wound to be fatal, you may then neglect the many resources available to heal victims of sexual violence, including a God who proved new life could come out of the worst suffering.

There will be many miserable moments when you might feel as if your sanity and life have been permanently destroyed. These feelings come and go. Your thinking may become distorted. Your emotions are raw and not always accurate. People you once thought of as friends may now be regarded as enemies, more so if you were assaulted by someone you knew. You may misinterpret or overreact to comments made by others that are meant to be helpful. Bible verses that once were comforting and positive may now seem offensive and negative. It might be beneficial to find a friend or a counselor who understands why you are having these reactions and can help you gain a proper perspective of what is happening.

It's tempting to blame the rape for every aggravation that comes along, however unrelated—your car won't start on a rainy morning, your only carton of milk is sour, you can't remember your secret code number at the automatic bank teller. Blowing these incidents out of proportion may help dissipate some of the anger you can't direct toward the assault. However, if you pile so much anger from other areas on top of your outrage over the rape, it can become too big of a problem for you to solve.

Refrain from making your sexual assault a permanent disability when God can bring hope and restoration into the most devastating circumstances. God is able to turn evil into good

(Genesis 50:20) and even make "a way in the desert and streams in the wasteland" (Isaiah 43:19). Suffering will come to all of us in this life. We as Christians can find meaning in our pain. God uses our afflictions to reveal his power and glory to an unbelieving world when our human nature sees nothing redemptive in the situation.

4. Use spiritual weapons to fight the negative consequences of rape. Prayer for God's miraculous and supernatural help should be our first response to any problem. Prayer is not positive thinking or the power of suggestion. It's calling upon the limitless ability of a Heavenly Father who hears us and answers our requests according to his will (1 John 5:14-15). Christians also have access to the Holy Spirit who "helps our weakness; for we do not know how to pray as we should, but the Spirit Himself intercedes for us with groanings too deep for words" (Romans 8:26 NAS).

The Word of God has an amazing transforming capacity to renew and restore. Following the desolation of a sexual attack, your sustenance and stability can hinge on reading, meditating on, and memorizing meaningful Bible verses. Christ stated in Matthew 4:4 that man shall not live by bread alone, but by every word that proceeds out of the mouth of God. Isaiah 26:3 promises, "You will keep in perfect peace him whose mind is steadfast, because he trusts in you." If you have difficulty reading the Bible because you are still too angry or confused, even Christian music, tapes, or literature can revive your spirit. But remember, some victims will need more time than others before they are open to any kind of spiritual nourishment.

A member of the clergy may be a good source of spiritual comfort, but some lack the time, training, and orientation to provide adequate, long-term counseling to a rape victim. The fact that most pastors are men may also be an obstacle for both the minister and the female victim. Some churches provide referral services to qualified agencies whose staff can help victims of sexual assault.

It's important to be in a group of believers who can pray for you and share your burden as commanded in Galatians

6:2. Your group doesn't have to know your specific problem if you are not comfortable sharing it. It would be advantageous, however, to carefully choose one or two people to be totally honest with about the rape. At least one confidant should be a mature Christian because a nonbeliever may not understand or value the spiritual recovery process. Women who feel isolated and misunderstood have a much harder time recuperating from a rape. Ecclesiastes 4:9 says, "Two are better than one . . . if one falls down, his friend can help him up. But pity the man who falls and has no one to help him up!"

Touching can also be a God-given therapeutic tool. Rape is a brutal physical attack which often leaves the victim feeling filthy and untouchable. Having a platonic friend who can hug you, rub your back, or stroke your arm can deliver support in a tangible way and penetrate barriers your mind has erected which inhibit healing.

5. Find acceptable outlets for your anger. The Bible teaches in Ephesians 4:26 that anger as an emotion is not wrong, it is the expression of anger that determines whether it is good or bad. Certainly it is normal to have strong feelings of hate, rage, and bitterness toward the rapist, however, a survivor's response can either help or hinder her recovery. Anger need not be destructive if constructively channeled. Resolving angry feelings affects your ability to function in all areas of your life.

The initial way you express your anger after a rape will be similar to the way you handle anger in other circumstances. One of the most common ways that women manage their anger is by turning it inward. When a woman gets mad, she has a tendency to victimize herself. When a man gets mad, he has a tendency to victimize others. This is mostly due to socialization where girls are raised to repress their temper; any expression of anger is considered unladylike, frivolous, or inappropriate. This is especially true for Christian women. For some it may be years before they allow their anger to surface.

When anger is internalized, it can have numerous physical and psychological repercussions. Victims of sexual violence often develop headaches, stomach ailments, eating disorders, depression, and suicidal tendencies. Sometimes there is so much rage and resentment, it's impossible to contain. Then it might be directed toward those closest to the victim in sudden, volatile, outbursts. If the person on the receiving end of this misdirected anger takes it personally, it can destroy the relationship. A less destructive way of discharging anger's power is to share it with an uninvolved third party, or with God.

Ellen Foster found that keeping a journal helped her discharge emotions, sort out what she was feeling, and see the progress she made over time. She also found an outlet in publishing articles and speaking to groups about her experience. Ellen used humor as another acceptable, effective method of defusing angry feelings. Humor helped her and those supporting her face disturbing emotions that otherwise might be too difficult to confront.

Physical exercise can be another outlet for angry impulses. Aggressive sports such as racquetball, aerobics, and tennis are excellent choices because they exert considerable energy. The biochemical changes that occur as a result of physical activity can also improve your emotional health.

After Elizabeth Green's rape, she found that the legal process helped vent some of her hostility. Even though the rapist received a light sentence, going to trial allowed her to direct her frustrations through a legitimate, orderly means. And she was satisfied that her assailant was registered as a sex offender, possibly sparing others from an attack.

6. Forgive the offender and leave the revenge to God. Forgiveness is the final, and probably most crucial, step in dealing with rape and its repercussions. For Christian victims, forgiveness is not only necessary for well-being, but commanded in Matthew 6:15. Psychologically, God has created us so that if we do not forgive others their transgressions God cannot forgive us our transgressions. Most secular books on rape don't talk about forgiveness because it is seen as unnecessary and impossible to achieve. Humanly, it is impossible to forgive a severe injustice such as rape, but God's grace imparted by the Holy Spirit can empower a victim to forgive.

An act of forgiveness by a rape victim cannot be rushed or orchestrated by others. Full forgiveness doesn't come quickly or easily. It is often a long process that is done in bits and pieces over a matter of years. There are deep emotions that cannot be easily dismissed; it will take time to reprogram feelings. It is insensitive and unrealistic for others to expect a wounded woman to move through the forgiveness procedure without great difficulty.

H. Norman Wright says, "Forgiveness is rare because it is hard. It will cost you love and pride. To forgive means giving up defending yourself. It means not allowing the other person to pay. It repudiates revenge and does not demand its rights. Perhaps we could say that it involves suffering."[1]

Forgiving does not mean that what happened to you did not matter or hurt. Forgiving never means excusing or condoning what the rapist did. It does not mean that the offender should not suffer the consequences of his actions under the law. *Forgiving means that you actively choose to give up your grudge in spite of how much you have been hurt.* Forgiving means that you release the power the offense has over your life and use it for more constructive purposes.

"Forgiveness takes place when love accepts—deliberately—the hurts and abrasions of life and drops all charges against the other person. Forgiveness is accepting the other when both of you know he has done something quite unacceptable."[2] Forgiveness is a process which restores severed relationships, resolves irreconcilable differences, and heals intolerable hurts.

The main unconscious motive for lack of forgiveness is vengeance. It's human to want to get even with someone, especially when the injury is horrendous and the transgressor shows no remorse. However, if you have any faith in God, personal vengeance is needless and disobedient. Paul says in Romans 12:17-21, "Do not repay anyone evil for evil. . . . Do not take revenge, my friends, but leave room for God's wrath, for it is written, 'It is mine to avenge; I will repay,' says the Lord. . . . Do not be overcome by evil, but overcome evil with good."

God will punish those who deserve it or he will show his divine grace and forgive them. Sometimes a rapist reaps natural consequences of his wrongdoing. Sex offenders in prison are often physically abused and discriminated against by other inmates. I received a letter from one convict who wrote he now understood and regretted what he had put his victim through after experiencing violent prison rapes. Another young man awaiting sentencing for a sex crime said that the shame and agony he had brought to his family was already punishment for his offense.

Jesus' death on the cross is our greatest example of forgiveness. God chose his only Son's death as the way of reconciling the world unto himself. God forgives us freely in Christ—he paid the full cost of forgiving. We are called to forgive as God has forgiven us. "Let all bitterness and wrath and anger and clamor and slander be put away from you, along with all malice. And be kind to one another, tender-hearted, forgiving each other, just as God in Christ also has forgiven you" (Ephesians 4:31-32 NAS).

Karen Burton Mains says, "Forgiveness is costly. It is an agony of submission. It is often entered into with tears. But it is only when we are willing to accept the sacrifice of suffering another offers to us that we can truly understand Christ's extravagant venture of forgiveness."[3]

7. *Forgive others, including yourself.* Just as you might have trouble forgiving the offender, you often cannot forgive others, however innocently they are involved in your violation. One woman resented her cousin because the rapist had approached both of them and the cousin got away. Another woman blamed her brother for introducing her to the man who later assaulted her. In yet another instance, an employer became the scapegoat after hiring a salesman who raped a co-worker. It also is easy to hate the jurors or judge if your offender is acquitted or if his conviction is overturned on a legal technicality.

Sometimes well-intentioned friends or family members may say things which are meant to be helpful, but sound hurtful to you. Comments such as, "You're young, you'll get over it," or "There are worse things that could happen to you" can build a wall between people instead of a bridge. Often a woman may not realize that her closest supporters are also immobilized by her crisis and she becomes embittered because they are unable to comfort her.

However deliberate the wrong done against you, if you fail to forgive, the resulting resentment can fracture a marriage, split a family, alienate a friend, jeopardize a job, or ruin your health. God foresaw the danger when he urged in Colossians 3:13, "Bearing with one another, and forgiving each other, whoever has a complaint against anyone; just as the Lord forgave you, so also should you" (NAS).

Many victims go to extraordinary lengths to blame themselves for their assault. This is easy to do when other people add to her self-incrimination. One woman berated herself for not having taken better care of her car, causing it to break down in an isolated area and leaving her vulnerable to an attack. Another felt stupid for going to a man's apartment on their first date. A third will never forgive herself for opening her door to an alleged repairman without first checking his identification. One rapist even made his victim feel at fault by saying she simplified the attack by wearing a dress.

Women, more often than men, assume liability for bad things happening to them. Men usually attribute their misfortune to chance or outside influences. Some victims never report their assault because they feel more to blame than their assailant. Others shoulder the responsibility for putting a man in prison or worry about the rapist's family while he is incarcerated. Whatever the circumstances of your assault, **you** did *not* deserve to be raped. You were the victim of a **violent** crime; you are not the person responsible. Even if you accidentally increased your chances of becoming a random target, you need not chastise yourself for something that in hindsight you would do differently. All the unforgiveness you keep inside hinders you from complete healing and living life to its fullest.

8. Confess your anger toward God, and ask his help to resolve it. Although God is incapable of doing anything wrong and therefore does not need to be forgiven, you may have repressed anger or bitter feelings toward him. You reason that if he is really God and truly benevolent, he wouldn't have allowed this to happen to one of his children. Especially when you lack support and involvement from your family and friends, you may feel that God has also abandoned you. In addition, you may think that a God who is most often characterized as male

95

cannot understand a woman's victimization; his "maleness" makes him an accomplice to the crime.

While anger toward God is sometimes a normal reaction, it's always undeserving since he claims in Psalm 103 to be perfectly fair, righteous, and loving in all that he does. He is never withdrawn or indifferent. In Isaiah 43:2, God promises to be with us in our suffering. You need to confess your anger toward God, and ask his help to resolve it; not for his sake, but for yours.

Deborah Roberts was nineteen years old when she felt called by God to devote her summer to an urban church ministry in Chicago. While delivering program materials one late afternoon in early July, Deborah was dragged into a tenement basement and brutally raped. Years later, Deborah wrote of her ordeal in the book *Raped*. With the help of her minister, Deborah was eventually able to resolve her anger toward God. In her book she quotes a portion of the sermon that helped her do this:

> The question, "How could God allow this to happen?" is best answered when we quit asking questions about God and go to Him in the midst of the tragedy, no matter how great, and trust Him to be the Good Shepherd who does not forsake His own. And it's there in His arms that somehow He brings meaning to us through it.
>
> What do we do when we don't understand God's answer? Are we to say, "God, you are unjust, maybe not righteous after all"? If we do that, then we remove ourselves from God's care; we wall ourselves out at the time of greatest need. We go through life cursing God and His people, rather than finding healing for our hearts, even if we cannot gain understanding for our heads.
>
> What I can't resolve, I take to God and leave with Him. I trust Him. I trust that He knows best. And if I have been a victim of some horrible evil, then in the midst of that tragic need, I need the Shepherd's care more than any other time.[4]

There is the tendency to think that rape is the one insurmountable problem outside of God's intervention. While rape is probably man's foulest outrage against a fellow human being, there is no situation where God is not involved and concerned. God hates all evil, especially rape. When his children suffer, he also suffers. However disgusting or shattering your circumstance, God has the power to repair and restore.

1. H. Norman Wright, *The Pillars of Marriage* (Ventura, Calif.: Regal Books, 1979), p. 164.
2. David W. Augsburger, *Cherishable Love and Marriage* (Scottsdale, Penn.: Herald Press, 1971), p. 146.
3. Karen Burton Mains, *The Key to a Loving Heart* (Elgin, Ill.: David C. Cook Publishing Co., 1979), p. 82.
4. Deborah Roberts, *Raped* (Grand Rapids, Mich.: Zondervan Publishing House, 1981), p. 127 and 129.

Victim recovery to a great extent depends on the willingness of family and friends to accept advice and personal counseling so that they can adequately resolve their feelings about the rape.

Carmen Germaine Warner

Without supportive responses from family, friends, church, and community, all too often victims remain victims.

Marie Marshall Fortune

8

"How Does This Affect My Family and Friends?"

CONTAGION

Rape is a crime that deeply influences not only the woman who is raped, but also her family members and other loved ones. The relatives and friends of a victim frequently experience many of the same psychological and physical side effects as the survivor; they become secondary victims. Rape is a social crisis: Anyone who has a significant relationship with the victim assumes her pain out of their concern and caring. But, in a compassionate, supportive environment most people will find that rape meshes with life's other unfortunate experiences.

PARENTS' BELIEF IN A JUST WORLD IS SHAKEN

No matter how old a rape victim is, her father and mother are also likely to be adversely affected by the assault. One of the primary roles of parents is to protect their children and see that they are safe. When a daughter is raped, the parents will often feel they have failed in safeguarding their family. Crisis counselors receive many calls from parents blaming themselves: "I should have taught her to fight back," "I never should have let her move into that part of town," "I should have insisted that she be home earlier."

Along with incriminating themselves, parents and other family members commonly blame the victim for the attack. Since older people more likely grew up thinking it was a woman's fault for getting raped, it may be hard for them to believe otherwise. This is particularly true if the woman was raped in what the parents see as compromising circumstances: she accepted a ride when her car ran out of gas; she attended a fraternity party where liquor was served; she left her bedroom window open on a hot night.

Even the most enlightened parents may make innocent comments ("He sure looks like a rapist," "Honey, why didn't you scream?") or, with hindsight, point out safety measures their daughter could have used. These responses increase their daughter's guilt. It is hard for them not to blame someone for the rape since it is intolerable to feel there's nothing anyone could have done to prevent it. The family's vulnerability is exposed and their belief in a just world is shaken.

Fathers of rape victims have an especially difficult time understanding what happened to their daughters. While most women focus primarily on the violent aspect of rape, the father and other men may think first of the sexual connotation. A father might withdraw because it's not only hard for him to think about a man sexually violating his daughter, it's discomforting to think about discussing such intimate matters with her.

Deborah Roberts says in her book *Raped*, "Telling everything to my father was much more difficult than telling the police. I had never before shared the private aspects of my life with him. Describing the intimate details of what had happened left me feeling naked in front of him. I would have to tell my story many times, but that time was the most difficult."[1]

Mothers, while not completely free from the misconceptions surrounding rape, can better understand that their daughter's assault was more terrorizing than titillating. Nobody except someone who has been raped can truly feel the horror the victim feels, but women can more easily sympathize because they live more with the fear of rape. For a time, the victim may be wary of all men, including her father, and rely on her mother and other women for comfort and understanding.

After their daughter is raped parents will often become overprotective by setting strict limits on her activities. They may be trying to insure her future safety or compensating for their own feelings of guilt or showing others that it was not their permissiveness which caused the assault. While their intentions might be good, their daughter may react by either rebelling against the restrictions or becoming so dependent she is unable to regain the ability to care for herself. When her freedom is curtailed, her anger at the rapist may be transferred to those confining her, breaking vital support relationships at a time when they are needed the most.

This was true for Cathy Campbell: "After I was raped, on one hand my mother said to forget the whole thing. On the other hand, she watched my every move. She started following me in the car when I went to school and calling friends' homes to check up on me. My younger brother and sister were allowed more freedom than I was. I guess I finally ran away to avoid being suffocated. But then I only got into more trouble."

HUSBANDS OFTEN REACT AS THE VICTIM DOES

Husbands and boyfriends often develop the same kinds of reactions as the victim—anger, guilt, fear, and self-blame. They also may need comfort and counseling. Yet because men are not supposed to be as weak as women, they might hide their pain and pretend to be unaffected, which the survivor may perceive as uncaring.

"How Does This Affect My Family and Friends?"

Because of cultural conditioning, men find it difficult to admit deep personal needs. They are reluctant to share their problems with counselors or family. If the spouse of a rape victim internalizes his feelings, family structure can fall apart. Therapy for the survivor alone seldom prevents severe difficulties in relationships.[2]

Her husband is usually the most important person in a married woman's recovery because of the sexual nature of rape. He can help her regain her pleasure in sex and her trust in men. Yet a husband can have his own struggles with sexual relations after an assault. He might be afraid that if others knew of his wife's rape, they would make jokes or see it as infidelity. He may know that rape is primarily an act of violence, yet still he can't help imagining another man forcing his spouse to have sex. In addition he might not understand why his wife is repulsed by physical contact with him. Again, both the husband and the survivor could benefit from talking with a professional or with other families of rape victims. They need reassurance that their reactions are normal and need not be permanent.

Sometimes men carry an enormous burden of guilt if they feel responsible for the attack. In some circumstances the rapist has violated the woman with the husband or boyfriend present. On other occasions a man may unwittingly leave a woman vulnerable to attack. A rapist assaulted dozens of women in the San Diego area by watching their homes in early morning until a man left for work or an early outing and then entering the residence through an unlocked entrance. Because men don't live with the daily fear of assault, they are usually not as conscious of safety precautions.

One of the initial impulses of a husband and other men in the victim's life is to get revenge. They automatically insist that someone pay for damaging their "property." While a woman is trained to suppress her anger, even the most peaceable man can turn into a vengeful maniac. Many buy a gun and try to capture or harm the rapist. Some husbands, brothers, or boyfriends of victims have served prison sentences for assault or attempted murder while the rapist went free.

Any attempts at reprisal will undoubtedly add to the victim's distress. On top of her own crisis, she must now be concerned about the safety of her loved ones. Her husband's overt fury might even be frightening if it reminds her of the terror of the assault. Furthermore, she may feel neglected if he is so preoccupied with his plans for retaliation or his continual anger that he ignores her immediate needs. A woman may unwisely try to protect her family from harm at the expense of her own healing if she senses that revenge is their main concern.

A husband, like a father, may become overly protective, suspicious, or jealous of the wife's activities. This is especially true if the rapist was an acquaintance rather than a stranger. The husband may feel that she's a poor judge of character or that she's simply not safe in her everyday surroundings. He may insist that she quit her job or that he take over any outside errands or that he drive her everywhere.

While it's normal for a woman to need sheltering the first few weeks after a rape, too much ongoing protection is defeating. A victim needs to rebuild her own internal sense of security and she can't if she's always watched, never allowed to go anywhere alone, or made to feel she's a prisoner. After the initial crisis is over, she has to have the freedom to begin functioning again on her own.

THE EXTENDED FAMILY IS DISRUPTED

A rape is usually disruptive for the entire extended family—siblings, children, in-laws, and other relatives of the victim. Daily routines and environment may be disturbed, harmonious family relationships may deteriorate, thus calling for major readjustments within the family structure. Loved ones become frustrated if they want to give support to the victim but do not know how to act or what to say. Or they may be too enmeshed in their own response to the rape to offer constructive help.

Brothers and sisters of a rape victim may resent the publicity, embarrassment, and preoccupation which the assault causes. Resentment increases if important events in the siblings' lives are ignored or forgotten because of the rape. Their schedules may also be carefully monitored as the parents' obsessive need to keep the survivor of rape safe spreads to the whole family.

Understandably, young children of the victim can be confused by the crisis. They sense something bad has happened but may be too young to comprehend the severity of rape. A child's sense of safety is shaken, more so if he or she were present during the attack or discovered their mother shortly afterwards when she was still badly shaken. What children imagine is usually worse than reality, so they need to be given an opportunity to know the facts. They also may need comfort and reassurance from other family members since their main source of comfort and protection—their mother—has pressing needs of her own.

Elizabeth Green's children were sleeping in another room during her attack. "They were victimized as much if not more than I was. First, even though they stayed in their beds, they undoubtedly heard my screams. Later they knew that the police had come and taken their mother away. And even though I tried to protect them from neighborhood gossip, they sensed something wicked and mysterious had happened to me. I think that they lost some of their childhood innocence during the whole ordeal and were forced to grow up too fast."

Older children can also be traumatized. They may feel extremely uncomfortable thinking about something as sinister and sexual as rape happening to their mother. Financial worries may plague the family if the rape necessitates medical or counseling expenses, or loss of income if the mother quits her job or both parents take a leave of absence. The victim may feel the need to change residence or locality, forcing children to adjust to new schools and new friends on top of dealing with the rape.

Sometimes rape divides families, especially when communication problems already exist. Some relatives may be very supportive of the victim while others doubt her story or blame her for the assault. Others may disagree about ways to help her. Family members are often ambivalent about pursuing prosecution, considering the further trauma and resultant publicity for everyone.

"While some of my family was understanding, others were unbelievably insensitive," Ann Crawford disclosed. "One relative actually confronted the psychologist who'd raped me, and of course he denied the whole thing. So this relative believed the rapist's word over mine. Another family member told me, 'A little sex never hurt anyone.' There are still unresolved differences not only between me and other relatives, but also among themselves. My recovery was definitely prolonged by my having to take time and energy from my own crisis to try and mediate family arguments concerning my assault."

FRIENDS ARE OFTEN MORE OBJECTIVE

While people experiencing other life crises use family as their primary source of support, rape victims often depend on alternate helpers such as friends, clergy, police, or medical personnel. Many women never tell their family, fearing their reaction or wanting to protect them from the pain of knowing. Friends or professionals, with less emotional attachment, can often extend more objective support.

A friend can also be a convenient outlet for the victim's bottled-up anger. She may have stifled her emotions with relatives because she didn't want to upset them. Or perhaps the victim is from a family that never allowed expression of angry feelings. An understanding friend, who doesn't take the fury personally, can be an invaluable release for the wounded woman's pent-up emotions. If a friendship can stretch to accommodate the victim's yelling, crying, and raging—and not be strained or severed—that relationship can be instrumental in her healing.

"Friends were invaluable to me in the first few months after my rape," Barbara Blake recalled. "My parents are dead and no relatives live nearby, so my neighbor came over in the evenings when I got off work so I wouldn't have to be alone. My ex-roommate came back to stay with me during the night. And a young man at my church started walking me home after services even though it was only two blocks. I was still frightened since the attack occurred so close by."

However, friends are not completely free from the effects of a rape. Some become uncomfortable hearing of their friend's assault because they are reminded of their own vulnerability. Others might be forced to recall a similar traumatic experience from their past which may have been one of the reasons why the victim confided in them in the first place.

It is troubling to watch a friend go through the rape trauma syndrome. She may be sad all the time, having lost interest in life and socializing. Her friends may feel neglected or they may grieve because she is not the same person she was before the rape. They want her to get back to normal for their sake as well as for her own. The victim's depression is contagious. Being around someone who is depressed can be a draining experience. It's easy for the supporter to become impatient with the rape survivor and wonder why it is taking her so long to recover.

While most women would automatically turn to another woman for comfort following a rape, some have reported that a male friend was remarkably sensitive and helpful after their assault. Others have forged a bond with a casual acquaintance such as a neighbor who came to their aid after the attack or a supervisor who was considerate of their workload limitations in the weeks afterwards. Many victims develop an ongoing phone relationship with an anonymous (only first names are used) rape crisis counselor working on a hotline. They request a certain counselor when they call, or they wait until their shift begins.

Even a stranger at the right time and place can be an important part of the progression in the recovery process, as in Ellen Foster's experience: "One night after I played a concert, I was feeling really bad. It had been two months since the rape and the legal process was beginning. A stagehand at the auditorium was helping me load my instruments into my car. He seemed so concerned about my mood that I ended up confiding in him. Those few minutes of his listening and consoling me are a memorable part of my healing."

HOW CAN OTHERS HELP?

The crisis of rape can bring a survivor and her supporters closer together. The victim of rape has been violated by another person. If her recovery is bolstered by others, it can neutralize the violation and reassure her of the trustworthiness of most people. The sustenance of others can give a woman the extra confidence necessary to face her fears, take risks, and rebuild her life.

Assisting someone in a crisis can be a rewarding experience in itself. A supporter may benefit as much from giving help as the hurting woman does in receiving it. The following ten suggestions are meant to aid those who want to help victims of rape:

1. *Be informed* about what services are available in your community for victims of sexual assault. Look in your telephone directory under "rape" or ask the operator for assistance. Find out which hospitals and police departments have staffs trained in rape trauma. Know the number of the nearest rape crisis hotline. Immediate crisis intervention can mean the difference between an effective resolution to rape or a lengthy, poor adjustment. Minutes of skillful support shortly after the crime can save the victim hours of professional counseling later.

2. *Be prepared* for extreme personality changes in the victim. She may show wide mood swings or be in a state of shock. For no apparent reason, she may burst into tears or have feelings of panic. She may also blame you for not protecting her from the attack. Allow her to release painful feelings without trying to calm her down (which is usually for your benefit, not hers). Don't attempt to erase her hurt or deny its significance before she is finished grieving.

3. *Be calm*, but not cold or indifferent. Helping a person in trouble requires extraordinary discipline and sensitivity. Those who comfort must focus on the victim's needs without imposing their own perceptions or suggestions. If she senses that her experience is upsetting you or that you would rather not discuss it at all, she may withdraw from your vital support. Rape crisis counseling is advisable, especially if those close to the victim are not comfortable dealing with the subject.

4. *Be sensitive* in probing for details of the rape; her privacy has already been violated. Don't expect or demand immediate, open communication about intimate aspects of the assault. Do not ask questions that indicate you are more interested in the specifics of the attack than in her feelings about it. Under no circumstances should you judge her behavior or doubt her story. She needs to know that you do not blame her for being in a situation that resulted in rape or for failing to resist the rapist. Never insinuate she could have prevented the attack by doing something differently. Making verbal threats toward the rapist in front of the victim may add to her trauma.

5. *Be cautious* about helping her too much. Do not be overprotective or treat her as if she is unable to decide what is best for herself. If you take over her decision making, you will be robbing her of her will and her dignity—similar to what the rapist did. You also might be encouraging her to develop an unhealthy dependency on you. Let her be the one to tell you she does not feel capable of making some choices. In particular, the decision to prosecute the rapist should be the victim's, after she is informed of all the pros and cons. No matter what she decides, she needs to feel that you will stick by her.

6. *Be careful* about physical contact with the victim. Some may want to be held and comforted, others do not want to be touched at all. Yet at the same time, she needs reassurance that you are not repulsed by her nor do you equate her rape with an act of infidelity or promiscuity. The husband of a rape victim especially needs to communicate that she is still desirable, without pressuring her to resume sexual relations before she is ready.

7. *Be available* to her needs as a person, not just as a rape victim. Although the assault is very much on her mind, it is not the only thing in her life. She may do a lot of crying, but she also needs to laugh. She might need help with simple everyday chores, but don't treat her as an invalid or overdo the cheery bedside manner. Family and friends should be discouraged from conspiring to distract the woman from the rape with a variety of activities. As much as possible, try to relate

to her as you did before the assault so she doesn't feel abnormal or contaminated.

8. *Be patient* with her progress. She needs to be allowed to go through the healing process at her own pace, however long it may take. Show that you find it justifiable and normal for the effects of her rape to be long-lasting. Never indicate that you think she's overreacting or that she was lucky something worse didn't happen. Validate what she feels, not how you think she should feel.

9. *Be discreet* about telling others of someone's rape. Never speak casually about what is shared in distress or said in confidence. If you solicit support from others, even the most sympathetic, without her knowledge or permission, her privacy is invaded. Although she needs others to pray for her, a request for prayer should be handled tactfully so she doesn't feel further stigmatized.

10. *Be encouraging* about her recovery. Assure her that she is not a failure, nor has she been singled out to suffer this indignity. She is one of thousands of women who are raped each year. Joining a rape survivor's support group can be therapeutic. If the woman is a Christian, she has the spiritual resources to be healed completely. Give her time, however, to resolve any confusion or anger with God before you talk about forgiving the rapist or positively integrating the rape into her life.

Is There Any Way to Make the Crisis Easier to Bear?

Rape doesn't wait for a convenient time to happen. A woman is often young, alone, helpless, and off guard when she is attacked. That's why a sexual assault is defined as a crisis: an event that is sudden and stressful, an event where a person's normal coping abilities are immobilized.

Is there a way that family and friends can make the crisis easier to bear for everyone involved? Yes, by using forethought and preparation. How people react in emergencies depends largely upon how well they have been trained to react. Families prepare for other disasters. Their homes are equipped with first aid kits, smoke detectors, and fire extinguishers. Individuals study cardiopulmonary resuscitation (CPR), the Heimlich maneuver, and what to do in an earthquake or a tornado.

Rape is a trauma requiring similar coping skills—the ability to quickly assess a situation and make proper decisions for immediate and long-term care. While many families have discussed rape prevention, few have talked about dealing with the ongoing repercussions of an actual assault. It is also important for people to be aware of their present attitudes toward rape in case someone close to them needs their future help. One victim never told her parents because she had once heard her mother comment, "A woman can't be raped if she doesn't want to be."

The relatives and friends of Ellen Foster and Barbara Blake were instrumental in their recoveries. Ann Crawford, Cathy Campbell, and Elizabeth Green were not as fortunate. In many ways their healing was hampered by responses of loved ones.

What makes the difference between groups and individuals who are supportive and those who are damaging? Three significant factors distinguished the families, friends, and helpers of the women whose recovery was expedited.

First, *communication* was already healthy between Ellen and Barbara and their helpers. A rape is an uncomfortable enough subject to broach but nearly impossible if openness does not already exist. Ellen and Barbara were used to sharing intense feelings in cell groups at church, with their roommates, and with relatives.

Secondly, the families that fared better had developed coping skills by *experiencing past crises or anticipating future ones.* Ellen's parents had immigrated to the United States having spent their youth in war-torn Germany. They were forced to learn how to live with adversity. While most people won't be confronted with as serious a misfortune, emotional muscle can be developed by working through a series of small stresses. When one consistently avoids frustrating circumstances or never confronts obstacles or rarely delays gratification, there is no opportunity to learn how to handle suffering. Gail

Sheehy, in her book, *Pathfinders*, says, "Rarely does creative endurance, or courage, become possible without the introduction of adversity."[3]

Thirdly, those who had an easier recovery were *altruistic people* before and after the rape. Their service to others not only took their minds off their own problems, but it also prepared them for trauma by experiencing coping techniques vicariously. Barbara had been a foreign missionary for many years. In serving others she mastered skills that enabled her to recognize and draw on resources in her own crisis. During her recovery, she wrote letters to newspapers and magazines educating others about rape. Later she urged her church to start a support group for victims. Many women, by volunteering at a local rape crisis center, gain awareness and empathy to help others and themselves in the event of an assault.

A crisis can bring out the worst in a person, but it can also extract the best. Survivors of rape often experience their crisis resolution as a maturing and toughening experience. They end up feeling less vulnerable and more capable of handling stress.[4] Coping with rape is not something that comes naturally to a woman or to her family and friends. However, it is possible to learn the right way to respond. When people understand what rape really is, how it affects a woman and her loved ones, and what their needs are afterwards, the trauma can be handled in a healthy, constructive manner.

1. Deborah Roberts, *Raped* (Grand Rapids, Mich.: Zondervan Publishing House, 1981), p. 44.
2. Susan Halpern, Dorothy J. Hicks, and Theresa L. Crenshaw, eds., *Rape: Helping the Victim* (Oradell, N.J.: Medical Economics Co., Book Division, 1978), p. 51.
3. Gail Sheehy, *Pathfinders* (New York: William Morrow & Co., 1981), p. 323.
4. Morton Bard and Dawn Sangrey, *The Crime Victims' Book* (New York: Basic Books, 1979) p. 155.

Rape can be as acceptable or unacceptable, as overt or covert as a society wants it to be.
                                                                Margaret Mead

The only thing necessary for the triumph of evil is for good men to do nothing.
                                                                Edmund Burke

9

"Why Is Rape So Prevalent?"

EPIDEMIC

There are no easy answers as to why forcible rape is the most frequently committed violent crime in America today.[1] A great many issues contribute to its prevalence: societal sexism, rampant pornography, apathy of the Church, media misrepresentation, cultural conditioning, and ineffectiveness of the legal system. The social institutions responsible for handling and reducing rape—the police, hospitals, and courts—are overwhelmed by the continual increase of sex offenses.

"Why Is Rape So Prevalent?"

Any solution to rape is multifaceted. Most people are confused by the complexity of the crime. Many feel that it is society that needs rehabilitation, not just the person guilty of an actual assault. While contemporary insight is leading to better understanding and treatment of victims, age-old damaging notions die slowly. In spite of the progress, we still have a long way to go before rape and its contributing causes are subdued and finally eliminated.

SOCIETAL SEXISM

The dominance of men and the inequality of sex roles in our society is thought by many to be the foundational cause of rape. Sexual violence is not an isolated phenomenon of "sick" males, but an integral part of an entire culture which oppresses women—physically, emotionally, politically, and economically. Rape will not be eliminated until the status of women in society is fundamentally improved.

Throughout history rape has been viewed as a special kind of crime, or no crime at all. Six hundred years ago rape was originally perceived as an offense against a man's "property" and that early concept continues to be the basis of today's rape laws. The higher the social or economic position of the victim's husband or father, the harsher the penalty for the rapist. The punishment for rape is still based on how valuable society views the victim. Research shows that the greater the socio-economic status of a rape victim, the more likely she will be considered credible. Like other forms of physical assault, rape should be defined and treated as an offense against a person, regardless of value, not against a commodity.

As previously stated, the underlying motive for rape is desire for power and control. Men use rape as an outlet by which they can release their pent-up feelings of powerlessness. As long as our society is divided between men as the wielders of power and women as a largely powerless class, victimization of females becomes increasingly possible. Susan Brownmiller in *Against Our Will* says, "Does one need scientific methodology in order to conclude that the anti-female propaganda that permeates our nation's cultural output promotes a climate in which acts of sexual hostility directed against women are not only tolerated but ideologically encouraged?"[2] Until this sexist attitude, which spawns violence against women, is abolished, there can be no lasting or widespread change.

PORNOGRAPHY IS WIDESPREAD AND INSTIGATIVE

Pornography is only one element contributing to the prevalence of sexual violence. But it is a significant element because it is so widespread and instigative. There is a growing amount of evidence linking the use of pornography to crimes against women and children. A flood of research by sociologists, psychologists, and law enforcement agencies during the past decade show that sexually violent fantasy material can alter the user's sexual attitudes, appetite, and behavior.[3]

The 1986 Attorney General's Commission on Pornography unanimously concluded that repeated exposure to violent and sexually explicit images can lead to unlawful acts of sexual violence.[4] The commission found a direct correlation between immersion in obscene matter and the increased likelihood of violent behavior toward women. Their findings suggest that a substantial number of sex offenders use pornography to start the process that triggers the crime. Dr. James Dobson, one of the commissioners, said, "Pornography is the theory; rape is the practice."[5]

Pornography exposes the observer to images that show sexual abuse and torture of women as positive and pleasurable experiences for the victim. In nearly every pornographic magazine or movie, the woman initially rejects the forceful advances of the male, but eventually becomes aroused, willingly submits, and begs for more. This leaves the user of pornography with the impression that aggressive sexual exploitation of women is acceptable and normal.[6]

Further evidence which supports the connection between rape and pornography are studies in which men were massively exposed to pornography. The majority of the participants began to view rape as a trivial crime or no crime at all. Most admitted that they would rape a woman if they thought they could get away with it. There was also a greater acceptance of the "rape myth"—the belief that women really want to be abused and enjoy being coerced into painful sexual acts.[7] Another study discovered a correlation between sex magazine readership and the rape rate. Researchers found that Alaska and Nevada had the highest readership of pornography in proportion to the population. Alaska and Nevada also lead all other states in incidents of rape.[8] (It is also interesting to note that the Las Vegas area, where legal prostitution flourishes, has one of the highest incidences of rape in the country. There are those who argue that rape would be eliminated if prostitution were legalized.)

Even without confirmation from secular research, from a biblical viewpoint, pornography, while not always illegal, is clearly immoral. Pornography not only dehumanizes and degrades women, but it leads to aggressive acts against them and violation of their personal rights. Randy Alcorn in his book, *Christians in the Wake of the Sexual Revolution* says, "Pornography is trash precisely because it treats people as trash. It is antiwomen, antichildren, antihuman, and anti-God, in whose image its victims are made."[9]

APATHY OF THE CHURCH

The Christian community, both collectively and individually, has contributed to the escalation of sexual violence because it has done so little to stop rape. While some Christians are concerned, rape abounds partly because so many Christians do nothing. The church, as a whole, is ignorant, unprepared, and oblivious to the problem of sexual assault. Satan has taken advantage of the church's uninvolvement to continue to attack Christians and non-Christians alike.

Additionally, the Christian community is almost wholly neglectful in teaching girls and women rape awareness and prevention. This gives church women a false sense of security and a harder time dealing with an actual assault. The Rape Crisis Center where I volunteer, which serves a city of more than a million people, receives hundreds of requests each year for speakers on rape. These requests come from businesses, schools, philanthropic groups, and even men's clubs, but hardly ever from a church. Some professionals feel that the number of persons in the Christian community who are victims of sexual abuse is extremely high because the church is naive, thus vulnerable.

The teachings of some churches can also contribute to women being victimized. Many groups of believers overly emphasize portions of Scripture that stress female submission to men and overlook verses which urge mutual submission. This can lead to a low view of women and encourage their being abused sexually.[10]

The church produces a sad predicament for the victim of sexual violence. Most pastors say they rarely or never have had a rape victim come to them for counsel. Because sexual assault is so extensive, they agree it was not because few church women were involved, but because the victim does not ask them for help. She senses, often correctly, that the collective church would respond to her with awkwardness and inappropriate assistance.

Would churches then be receptive to a presentation to better understand the problem? A number of pastors say no. Because few victims have come forth, the clergy concludes it is not a concern within their congregation.

One Baptist pastor summarized his feelings: "It's not that I don't want to help rape victims—I just don't know how. It's a unique counseling situation that we never learned in seminary. I would have to refer her to a specialist I have taken time to investigate. Ideally it would be better to help her within the church family. However, I know of only a few churches nationwide that provide this service."

Seldom does a clergyman have the time, training, or aptitude to counsel victims of sexual assault.[11] Yet many hesitate to research and recommend secular resources. Ministers often mistrust social service agencies with the needs of their congregation.[12] This is especially true in the area of sexual violence since the majority of victim assistance programs and literature available on the subject have been initiated by feminists.

Likewise, rape crisis centers are frequently skeptical about the ability of pastoral staffs to deal effectively with a victim since the church has remained uninformed and uninvolved. This lack of cooperation usually leaves the woman needing help caught in the middle. Many times she is forced to choose between spiritual and secular resources or no help at all when she could benefit from both.

Rape is a crime against God and humanity. The body of Christ is called to express God's love and healing to anyone experiencing grief and pain. Pastors and lay people need to recognize the rape victim as an individual who deserves their most compassionate and educated response. As salt of the earth, Christians have a unique opportunity and God-given responsibility to stem evil wherever it abounds. Apathy and ignorance give women the impression that sexual violence is the unmentionable sin.

MEDIA REPRESENTATION

The media plays a significant role in perpetuating sexual violence because it represents a major source of learning and socialization for most people. Rarely is an accurate picture of rape portrayed in movies, television, print, or music. When people, especially children, form their concept of rape from the entertainment world, they have little idea of what to expect in the real world.

Victims of rape are stereotypically presented as a young, ravishing woman who is either too much in shock to resist her attacker or who struggles and protests in a helpless, submissive manner. In the rare cases when a woman does successfully defend herself, she is characterized as unfeminine or Amazon-like.

The rapist is often depicted as a sex-starved psychotic who can't help himself or as an otherwise normal young man whose domineering mother or rejecting lover pushed him into abnormal behavior. The moral of the story is that if women were just better women—as mothers, wives, girlfriends and potential victims—then the problem of rape would go away.

The media also stereotypes police officers and the legal

investigation. A policeman is often either callous and bungling or he is macho and magnetic, solving the case and convicting the rapist in fifty-one televised minutes. In reality, police departments are mostly comprised of committed, hardworking individuals involved in lengthy, frustrating rape investigations.

Another common misrepresentation of the media is the neglect to show the involvement and availability of Rape Crisis Centers. If victim advocates are shown, it is usually as radical, angry, unreasonable women. Such depictions unfairly distort the work of these trained and dedicated volunteers. And an opportunity is missed to provide a much-needed public service in informing the community of the existence of Rape Crisis Centers.

Myths contributing to the escalation of rape are also prevalent in popular forms of music. Since people hear a song many more times than they see a specific movie or television program, the false concepts are even more deeply embedded. Rock music, especially, contains clearly sadistic and pornographic lyrics which teach listeners that sexual violence is commonplace, acceptable, and even desirable for the woman.

This flood of misinformation in print, recordings, and film dulls our senses to the brutality of rape. The bizarre situations shown form our belief that it could never happen to the average, ordinary person. When rape is erroneously presented without lasting trauma, we are less compassionate toward the victim. When the rapist continually escapes harsh consequences, people are subliminally taught that there is nothing so bad about men forcing their will on women.[13]

CULTURAL CONDITIONING INFLUENCES SEXUAL VIOLENCE

Prevailing sexual attitudes and cultural values of a society greatly influence the rise and fall of sexual violence. The American people are immersed in sex and aggression. Often the two are combined in advertising, sports, and entertainment and are rewarded with money, power, and status. A culture perpetuates whatever it values. In societies where sex and male aggression are not emphasized and reinforced, rape is uncommon.[14]

119

Sex-role stereotyping can also create a climate for sexual violence. Boys are typecast as dominant and conquering; girls are expected to be passive and coy. Aggressiveness is an approved trait in men, but discouraged in women. These attitudes not only encourage men to force sex on a woman, but often prevent a woman from realizing she can resist.

Traditional dating rituals can also leave a girl susceptible to assault. The majority of rapes are perpetrated by someone the woman knows, frequently in a dating situation. Commonly, the boy will ask the girl out and pay for the expenses of the outing. Often it is assumed that she owes him something for his time and money; the more he spends on her, the more she owes. The woman is also saddled with the responsibility for saying no to any unwanted sexual advances and also to convince the man that she really does mean no.

Ironically, even American etiquette can set the stage for rape. Because women are socially trained to be ladylike and well-mannered, a rapist will often pre-test a woman to see how cooperative she would be. Women often jeopardize their own safety for fear of making a scene or being considered rude. They are conditioned to smile and be polite under the most uncomfortable circumstances. While the desire to help others and believe the best of people are ordinarily considered virtues, women who display these qualities are likely to be targeted by a rapist as an easy victim.

Theodore Bundy, the notorious rape-murderer, lured many victims into his trap by pretending to have a broken arm and asking them to help him carry or lift something. Unfortunately, we don't live in an ideal world where we can trust everyone. Rapists have been known to pose as policemen, accident victims, service personnel, and even women. It is imperative that women take precautions, however foolish or discourteous they seem, for their own safety.

LEGAL INEFFECTIVENESS

In America the state takes little or no responsibility for the welfare of crime victims. Although one of the government's major roles is the protection of its citizens, the criminal justice system is more concerned with the rights of the accused. Nowhere is this more evident than in cases of rape. While public pressure has resulted in some progress, there are still many problems that rape victims face within the criminal justice system.

Since a rapist is just as likely to be acquitted as convicted by a jury, prosecutors are reluctant to spend time and energy on a rape case unless it's airtight. Since the district attorney is a publicly elected official, it can be professionally detrimental to lose too many cases. As one lawyer said, "There is no such thing as too much evidence in a rape trial."

This caution is passed down to the police. Neither do they want to expend hours investigating a case that will never come to trial. The police may then discourage the survivor from reporting if it does not look like a prosecutable case.

Even if a rapist is charged, he has the right to post bail. Many remain free for months until the trial, continuing their sexual assaults and threatening previous victims and their families.[15] Often there is no room on the court schedule for his hearing, thus he is allowed to plea bargain for a lesser offense and is let off with probation.

The legal system is overburdened and overcrowded with rapists of all ages. A sizable majority of sex offenders begin their crimes during adolescence. Even elementary school-age gang rapes are being increasingly reported. Treatment for all but the most serious juvenile offenders is nonexistent. The incarcerated adult rapist does not fare much better. Of the 5,000 registered sex offenders in California, less than 1 percent receive psychological counseling in prison. Many professionals feel that treatment programs for rapists are too controversial, expensive, and ineffective.

The end result of the legal system's inadequacy is that the world becomes a safer place for the criminal, but not for the victim. Men learn that they are free to rape because the courts are powerless to stop them. Those who are convicted serve an average of three years. One famous California rapist only served eight years for raping a teenaged girl, chopping off her forearms, and leaving her for dead.[16] When they are released,

80 percent of convicted rapists will commit another crime, mostly sex offenses.

Societal sexism, pornography, church apathy, media misrepresentation, cultural conditioning, and an ineffective legal system are some of the influences contributing to the rise of sexual violence. Under the guise of freedom of the press, separation of church and state, and humanistic pursuit of happiness, society allows the moral climate to deteriorate. As a result, those less able to defend themselves become increasingly victimized. Dr. Carmen Germaine Warner, a specialist in the field of sexual violence says that rape "will be reduced only if enough people are willing to admit that the present situation is intolerable and are courageous enough to initiate widespread social change."[17]

1. Susan Griffen, *Rape: The Politics of Consciousness* (San Francisco, Calif.: Harper & Row, 1979), p. 4.
2. Susan Brownmiller, *Against Our Will*, (New York: Simon & Schuster, 1975), p. 444.
3. Jerry R. Kirk, *The Mind Polluters* (Nashville, Tenn.: Thomas Nelson Publishers, 1985), p. 53.
4. Michael J. McManus and others, *Final Report of the Attorney General's Commission on Pornography* (Nashville, Tenn.: Rutledge Hill Press, 1986), p. 40.
5. Tom Minnery, ed., *Pornography: A Human Tragedy* (Wheaton, Ill.: Tyndale House Publishers, 1986), p. 40.
6. Marie Marshall Fortune, *Sexual Violence: The Unmentionable Sin* (New York: The Pilgrim Press, 1983), p. 234.
7. Minnery, p. 72.
8. Kirk, pp. 51-52.
9. Randy C. Alcorn, *Christians in the Wake of the Sexual Revolution* (Portland, Ore.: Multnomah Press, 1985), p. 126.
10. Earl D. Wilson, *A Silence to be Broken* (Portland, Ore.: Multnomah Press, 1986) p. 126.
11. Fortune, p. 132.
12. Ibid, p. 131.
13. Linda Tschirhart Sanford and Ann Fetter, *In Defense of Ourselves* (Garden City, New York: Doubleday & Co., 1979), p. 16.
14. Carmen Germaine Warner, ed., *Rape and Sexual Assault* (Germantown, Md.: Aspen Systems Corp., 1980), p. 283.
15. Joy Satterwhite Eyman, *How to Convict a Rapist* (New York: Stein & Day Publishers, 1980), pp. 9-10.
16. Rapist-mutilator Lawrence Singleton was released after serving eight years on a fourteen-year sentence. However, California state authorities were unsuccessful in their attempts to parole Singleton in more than a half-dozen communities because of public opposition. He was finally placed on the grounds of San Quentin prison for his own protection. While not incarcerated, he has twenty-four-hour supervision and an armed parole officer accompanies him on any excursions outside of San Quentin. The state pays Singleton's expenses.
17. Warner, p. 297.

This refusal to face the fear of rape is one of the major factors contributing to women's collective vulnerability to attack.

Marcia E. M. Molmen

There are only two ways to approach life— as a victim or as a gallant fighter—and you must decide if you want to act or react. . . . A lot of people forget that.

Merle Shain

10

"How Can We Stop Rape?"

———————————————————

THE CURE

R ape is a very real fear for all women, but rape is not inevitable.

However, the crime is rapidly escalating because too many women are too frightened by the idea of rape to do anything about it. While no woman can make herself rape-free in our culture, too many victims need not have been victims at all. Too afraid to face the possibility of rape, many ignore the risk and hope for the best. There is a saying, "What you don't know won't hurt you." In the case of rape, what you don't know *can* hurt you. Prevention offers us the opportunity to take the offensive against sexual violence, instead of waiting in dread for it to happen. We must realize it is entirely possible to greatly reduce our chances of becoming a victim.

Women can help reduce the possibility of rape in several ways. The primary objective is to keep a woman from circumstances where an assault might occur.

HOW TO RECOGNIZE A RAPIST

The first way to reduce one's chances of being victimized is to recognize characteristics in men that make them potential abusers. While it is impossible to categorize a typical rapist—he may exhibit none of these traits or he may display all of them and not be a rapist—many show one or more of the following warning signs.

- Hostility when people say no to him or he doesn't get his way—especially when he reacts with verbal or physical violence.
- An exaggerated sexist or supermacho attitude, calling women demeaning names, ordering a woman about as if she were an object rather than a person with her own wishes and feelings.
- Talks or acts as if he knows you more intimately than he does. Uses a degree of familiarity that is not appropriate by telling crude jokes, using vulgar language, asking personal questions, staring, "playfully" tickling or tousling, standing or sitting too close.
- Handles normal everyday frustrations with childish behavior such as temper tantrums, shirking responsibility, making excuses, or blaming others.
- Excessive possessiveness or jealousy in relationships with women. Demands complete control, even dictating what these women can wear or who they can see.
- Boasts about his sexual prowess, considers himself a "lady's" man, but actually has an immature or distorted view of sexuality.
- An underdeveloped conscience, either doesn't

know right from wrong or doesn't care. Defiant toward authority, particularly the criminal justice system.

- Uses drugs or alcohol, tries to get others to partake. These substances often contribute to violent behavior.
- Reads pornography, frequents adult bookstores or X-rated movies.
- Tries to get a woman alone or in a situation where she is in a poor position to assert herself such as encouraging her to get drunk or driving in a remote area. He may use his position of authority (i.e. an employer or a teacher) to get a woman alone.
- A history of violent behavior or a criminal record for aggravated assault or sex offenses.

Never assume that *anyone* is beyond suspicion by virtue of his community involvement, strong religious beliefs, or respected position. Go with your instincts; if a man's actions or remarks make you uncomfortable, politely but firmly resist immediately. Many women lose this initial opportunity to escape because they are afraid of appearing rude or looking silly if no harm was meant. It is better to be mistaken than to be raped.

WHAT INCREASES THE LIKELIHOOD OF RAPE?

A second way to limit the likelihood of an attack is to examine your own behavior. Statistics show that women are more likely to be victimized if they display one or more of these three characteristics: vulnerability, unawareness, or isolation. Follow these recommendations to lessen your risk of appearing a suitable target:

1. Don't appear vulnerable. A rapist hunts for a woman who looks weak, fragile, and helpless. He judges her by her susceptibility, stature, and stride—not her sexiness. Young girls, senior citizens, or disabled persons are especially vulnerable, but no woman should neglect body language as an integral aspect of self-defense.

Unconsciously, our movements and gestures telegraph our

thoughts, feelings, and perceptions. Confident behavior and an erect, purposeful walk transmit signals of strength and self-respect. If a woman shows signs of being alert, assertive and self-reliant, the rapist will probably search for an easier victim. He doesn't want to risk attacking someone who might be able to take care of herself.

Often a rapist will test a woman's vulnerability by first violating her personal space. He may pretend to touch her body unintentionally or make a lewd remark to gauge her reaction. He also might try to gain entrance to her car or home by claiming to be ill or lost, needing to use the phone. If she acquiesces to this initial advance, the rapist will undoubtedly have found his victim.

The more generally assertive a woman is, the less chance she will be targeted. Most women would profit from reading a book on assertiveness or enrolling in a self-defense course that teaches attitudinal preparation as well as physical preparation; defending yourself requires more mental knowledge than physical skill. A woman who knows self-defense is less likely to need it.

2. *Be aware.* The majority of rapists plan their assaults in advance by observing their victim over a period of time. Most women are so preoccupied with their everyday lives that they do not notice a potential assailant until the attack is imminent. Also, women do not follow the same precautions during the daytime as they would at night, so they might be more unaware. In Hawaii a series of rapes was committed by a man pegged "The Bus Stop Rapist." When caught, he admitted his method for choosing his victim: He would find a woman waiting alone at a bus stop then would drive around the block several times assessing her. If she was attentive and noticed him, he would pass her by. But, if she was filing her nails or rummaging through her purse, or otherwise preoccupied, it gave him the opportunity to stop and force her into his car.

A woman should always remain aware of her surroundings, the people with whom she comes in contact, and the situations that do not seem quite right. She should never ignore her instinctive feelings of danger—they are usually right. By remaining alert to the possibility she could be victimized, a woman eliminates the rapist's advantage of surprise.

3. *Avoid being isolated.* If a rapist finds a woman in an isolated environment, her chances for escape are significantly reduced. This is why hitchhiking is so dangerous. A disabled automobile is also a vulnerable position for a woman driving alone. Every woman should carry a "Call Police" banner (available in many stores), which she can display if her car breaks down. If possible a woman should avoid any situation where she is alone with a man she does not know well. Rapists look for unsuspecting victims on deserted streets, empty public restrooms, or vacant laundromats. Convicted rapists have admitted spending hours, or even days, searching for their isolated prey.

Even when all possible precautions have been taken, there may still be threatening situations when some method of self-defense is necessary. Rape prevention experts hold conflicting opinions regarding which tactics work. The best advice is that your course of action should depend on you, on the rapist, and on the situation. A woman should know her options and then respond in whatever way she feels is appropriate.

AVOIDING RAPE

Prevention can also help a woman deal with an actual attack. One's chances of being targeted by a rapist can be significantly reduced by following a list of safety precautions and security measures. These commonsense safeguards are applicable to protecting a woman from any violent crime, including rape, and are available from most police departments or the National Center for the Prevention and Control of Rape.[1]

While there are no specific instructions guaranteed to work in every circumstance, these are suggestions that may help you avoid being raped or injured:

1. *Plan ahead.* The panic that overcomes many women at the onset of an attack is largely due to a lack of mental preparation. When a woman has no idea of what to do next, she becomes totally helpless. This gives the rapist the initial

advantage. Even the simplest strategy is better than no plan at all.

Evaluating defensive measures beforehand can significantly improve your chances of resisting or surviving an attack. All women should contemplate what their approach might be given differing sets of circumstances. Also, studies have shown that victims who had a defense strategy in mind before the rape occurred recovered more quickly from its traumatic aftereffects than those who did not.

2. *Try to remain calm.* Calmness can help subdue an attacker; hysterics may aggravate him. This is where your mental preparedness is invaluable. We're all creatures of habit and we react, for the most part, how we have been trained to react. A threatened woman needs time and composure in order to evaluate the situation and plan an escape if possible. She cannot take effective action or read the rapist if she is emotionally unstable. The most important thing is to stay in control and see if the right moment to resist presents itself.

Pray for wisdom and protection. While screaming is a common response, it is usually useless unless someone is nearby to help. And it may put the woman in further danger if the attacker tries to silence her. The rapist is likely to be just as frightened as you are. If your self-control can gain his confidence and ease his fears, you may lessen the certainty or severity of an assault.

3. *Treat the rapist as a human being.* People tend to live up to the way others act toward them. Be careful to condemn the rapist's behavior, not him as a person. Calling him degrading names may cause his conduct to degenerate further. While it won't be easy to treat an assaulter as a human being, it may ignite a spark of compassion in him for your benefit. When you behave humanely toward him, it will be harder for him to see you as a nameless, faceless object.

A group of convicted rapists was asked what their victims could have done to prevent the attack. The overwhelming response was to make them see her as a real person with real feelings and understand how damaging the assault would be for her. When they could not depersonalize the woman and distance themselves emotionally from her suffering, they did not rape.

While just talking is not always successful, particularly if the rapist is drunk or on drugs, conversation may give you time to think of an escape or increase the chances of help arriving. At the very least, conversing with the attacker may provide some information for the police to catch him.

4. *Use your imagination.* By analyzing the rapist's personality and the circumstances of the assault, some women have avoided rape with passive resistance. This includes pretending to be sick or pregnant, fainting, reciting Bible verses, vomiting, urinating, or acting mentally disturbed. It is important to choose a strategy suited to your personality and situation. A poor actress can anger the rapist if he senses that he is being lied to. Don't attempt something so totally out of character that you can't be convincing.

While some women have successfully witnessed to their attackers, others have placed themselves in worse jeopardy by mentioning God. If you have another plan in mind and are sensitive to the rapist, you can change your tactics if they're not helping the situation. Unfortunately, there is no foolproof method that will work in all cases; each rapist and each circumstance is different. But even when all maneuvers fail, there is satisfaction in knowing you did something to resist.

5. *Be careful about using physical resistance.* Interviews with convicted rapists reveal that about half of them let their victims go when they screamed and struggled. The other half stated that the struggle caused them to brutally beat or kill their victims. Rapists are generally unstable people. If a woman starts aggressively defending herself, the rapist will likely reciprocate. Once violence is introduced, there may be no turning back, and the winner is usually the more violent party.

It is difficult for most women to effectively fight off an attacker without proper training. Even with training, many women are uncomfortable with the idea of hurting another person. If a woman is proficient in self-defense, it can be very effective if she practices to keep her skills honed. She should never be overconfident about her ability to defend herself, especially when there is more than one rapist or when weapons are involved. The most important thing is surviving the rape.

Physical resistance is generally recommended in three circumstances: when safety is nearby, so that yelling and fighting will bring help; when the attacker is an acquaintance not prone to violence; when a woman is in immediate danger of losing her life.

6. *Use extreme caution when confronted by an armed rapist.* Most rapists verbally threaten a victim's life, but if he displays a gun or other lethal weapon, you must take his threats more seriously. His behavior is hard to predict. You don't want to do anything to turn a probable rape into a possible murder.

Most experts agree that carrying a weapon for self-defense is unwise. Guns, knives, and spray chemicals can be taken and used against you. Besides, carrying a concealed weapon is illegal in many areas. An easily accessible whistle or siren can provide some protection.

Cooperate to avoid serious injury or death. Not all rape can be prevented. It is foolish to fight unto death to preserve your honor. If no self-defense ploy is successful and the sexual violation is inevitable, you could bargain with an attacker for a quick release without injury in exchange for your cooperation. Meanwhile, memorize details of the assault and a thorough description of the rapist to give to the police.

Submitting to a rape does not mean you consented. You should never blame yourself for anything you did, or didn't do, to survive an assault. Rape is a crime—whether or not a woman resists. No matter what approach a woman chooses during an assault, she should never have to apologize for the outcome. It is *always* the rapist who did something wrong, not the victim.

How Men Can Help

Preventing rape would be simpler for women if men also cooperated. Not every man is a rapist. It is partly because each individual rapist commits so many assaults that rape is rampant. However, very few men are working to abolish rape, and this is another reason why rape continues. Nearly all the progress against sexual violence has been initiated by women.

The enormous resources of American men—intellectual, political, and economic—would make the eradication of rape easier. While the subject of rape may make men feel uncomfortable, ashamed, or defensive initially, many men would awaken to the reality of violence against women and take action if they understood rape and knew how to help. These suggestions are for those men willing to get involved.

1. *Realize that rape is not just a concern for women.* It's a human plight affecting marriages, families, and entire communities. Men who have been victimized would be more comfortable reporting if rape were not perceived as only happening to women.

2. *Take rape seriously.* Don't tell jokes about rape or make rapist remarks. Don't try to scare women by not identifying yourself on the phone or by covering the peephole on the door so she can't see who is knocking. Poking fun at a serious subject can relieve embarrassment and frustration, but it can also encourage others to take lightly a cruel and violent act.

3. *Understand that your reaction to rape is different from a woman's.* A man's response to a loved one's rape will likely be anger and a murderous fury. A woman is usually more terrified. Men find it hard to understand why a woman did not fight back. Men more than women envision rape as forced sex rather than a life-threatening act of violence.

4. *Help victims of rape.* Volunteer on a rape crisis hotline. Most are understaffed and almost all counselors are women. Calls from male rape victims are increasing. They may need a man to accompany them to the hospital or police station. Sometimes the husband or father of a victim, or even the victim herself wants help from a masculine perspective. In some areas, a hotline for potential rapists is operative and needs ongoing support.

5. *Be aware that you are a perceived threat to many women.* Rape has given a bad name to all men. A woman will usually view courtesy and friendliness from a strange man with suspicion.

Obviously assessing her appearance, moving suddenly, or touching her without permission will add to her learned caution of men. Give a woman time, reason, and space to trust you.

6. *Be conscious of security precautions.* Some husbands are careless about locking doors and leaving enough gas in the car for their wives. Because of the persistent threat of sexual violence, women must live with hundreds of safety measures that may seem excessive to men. Do not, however, become overprotective so that a woman feels unable to take care of herself.

7. *Educate your children about rape.* Teach them the truth about sexual violence. Make sure they are comfortable enough with the topic to tell you if they are victimized. When children start dating, teach your daughter how to say no to unwanted sexual advances. Make sure that your son doesn't think that when a woman says no, she really means yes. We desperately need a generation of men and women not afraid to communicate with each other about rape.

8. *Pray about your involvement.* God may be calling you to be a spokesman in your church or community on sexual violence. Some may misunderstand your concern while others will admire your courage. While there are secular men's organizations opposing rape, there are no Christian ones. Christian men especially have the resources to help victims. Someone you love will likely become a victim or may already be one without your knowledge.

How Communities Can Help

When individuals get involved in preventing rape, conditions for rape victims improve. As more and more people join in the fight against sexual violence, the crime of rape can be successfully combated. These are some suggestions for individual and group involvement.

1. *Join with others to start, operate, or expand the services of a rape crisis center in your area.*

2. *Work to raise public awareness about rape* by distributing educational literature. Sponsor workshops on prevention.

Urge your local media to report sexual violence responsibly, without sensationalism.

3. *Lobby for changes in the criminal justice system.* Write politicians concerning unfair rape legislation. Examine police and medical procedures for proper victim care. Attend a sex crime trial to see how cases are handled in your town. Become familiar with the voting record of elected officials on women's issues. Publicly demonstrate to protest an unfavorable decision made by a judge. Encourage increased funding for rape-related projects.

4. *Fight pornography.* Lend your support to an established group opposing obscene material. Organize a boycott or picket stores which sell pornography. Put pressure on government representatives to enforce penalties against the distribution of smut.

5. *Participate in a neighborhood organization.* Banded together, neighbors can help each other deal with the threat of rape by printing information about rapists working in the area, holding meetings on preventive strategies, designating houses as safe havens for women in trouble, and reporting any suspicious activity on their street.

6. *Urge your school or place of employment to hold safety awareness programs.* Check out what measures are being taken on the job or on the campus to keep women safe. Insist on adequate outdoor lighting at night and security surveillance when workers or students are vulnerable.

7. *Report any sexual harassment, rapes as well as attempted rapes, lewd conduct, or obscene behavior.* Crude remarks, inappropriate touching, and insisting on helping a woman are favorite techniques for testing victims. If you don't pass the test, the rapist will likely go on to rape someone else.

WHAT CHURCHES CAN DO

Churches, as well as communities, have both the opportunity and responsibility to effect change in the area of sexual violence. The body of Christ wields tremendous power. If congregations are not willing to be part of the solution, they are likely to become part of the problem.

1. *Recognize that women in the church are particularly susceptible to sexual assault because, as a whole, they are uninformed and unprepared.* Satan undoubtedly takes advantage of this naiveness to attack Christians.

2. *Give pulpit time to the issue of rape.* Pastoral references can set the mood for proper attitudes and effective actions of the whole congregation. Include sermons on healing as well as non-biblical aspects of the problem, such as victim services, legal injustices, and rape preparedness.

3. *Instigate church programs to educate people of all ages.* Literature, audio-visuals, and speakers are available from rape crisis centers, police departments, hospitals, and social service agencies. A parish's discomfort and fear can be reduced as information is presented and discussed.

4. *Install and use security devices on church buildings.* Many times women are there alone, but they neglect to secure the premises because they feel safe in God's house. Church women also sometimes overlook inappropriate behavior in a man if he is a member of their church when they should use the same caution with any male.

5. *Urge the pastoral staff and select members of the congregation to train in crisis intervention and then make members aware that there are people ready and able to help a rape victim.*

6. *Provide a healing environment for survivors of sexual assault.* Brothers and sisters in Christ have a unique calling and God-imparted capacity to provide a loving, non-judgmental acceptance, answers to pain and suffering, and prayers for restoration to rape victims.

RAPE CAN BE ELIMINATED

When a social concern such as rape has been ignored and distorted for centuries, you don't change or solve the concern in just a few years. However, victims of sexual violence are far better off today than they were only ten years ago. In fact, when you consider how difficult change is in a society as complex as ours, the progress made on behalf of rape victims during the past decade is astounding.

One of the most significant advances is the opening of nearly one thousand rape crisis centers across the country. Most centers are operated by volunteers interested in helping victims and putting a stop to rape. These advocates offer twenty-four- hour-a-day support for survivors of rape and their families. Many centers also provide community education programs, self-defense classes, legal assistance, and referrals to qualified medical and psychological services. Nearly nonexistent a dozen years ago, these organizations serve as prime examples of what can be done to improve victim care. Many of these centers exist on private and public donations and are always in need of additional volunteers and funding.

Another major advancement is the hospital procedure for the sexually assaulted. Until a few years ago, victims were treated by hospital personnel who were medically, but not psychologically or legally trained to conduct examinations for evidence. Sometimes the evidence was improperly collected or overlooked, making prosecution more difficult.

Now numerous hospitals in nearly every state have specially trained doctors and nurses to treat sexual assault victims. The need for privacy is also better understood and some medical centers have a separate waiting room or private entrance for rape survivors. These days a woman is allowed to have a friend or a trained advocate with her during the evidenciary exam instead of a male police officer. Most areas now provide reimbursement for medical expenses incurred by a victim injured in a sexual assault. In the past she had to pay her own hospital bills. Unfortunately, these recently acquired rights may not be enforced if a woman doesn't know how to ask for them. Enlightened people are needed to help educate others.

Lastly, the criminal justice system—from the initial police contact all the way to the courtroom—has made tremendous strides in improving the treatment of survivors of sexual violence. Many local police departments now have special rape crisis teams. A victim can also request that a female officer or a nonuniformed officer in an unmarked car call at her home to ensure privacy. While a woman will still probably face a unique set of responses when reporting an assault, many positive changes have emerged to make prosecuting a rape less of an ordeal.

During the 1970s an enormous amount of legislation affecting rape was passed by almost every state. While some states made only minor changes, many completely rewrote their laws governing rape. One important revision in most states makes rape a crime even if penetration did not occur. Many jurisdictions now define rape as any attempted or completed nonconsenting contact with the sexual organs, including breasts and buttocks. This major victory and others could not have been won without the grassroots efforts of ordinary people who lobbied, signed petitions, demonstrated, or otherwise rallied on behalf of rape victims everywhere.

However, the most perfect rape laws, strictly enforced, will not be enough to stop or even abate rape. Preventing rape is not just a matter of following safety rules and incarcerating rapists. All efforts to abolish rape must be backed up with a change in society's attitude toward rape to have any real impact. Sexual assaults against women are not insulated occurrences. They are part of the social fabric in which sexist attitudes, economic and legal inequalities, exploitation of women's bodies, and the condonation of violence are all interwoven.[2] In order to effectively stop sexual violence, rather than just deflect the rapist to another individual or community, we must alter the underlying social structure which produces it. Changing such attitudes is not easy, nor does it happen overnight, but like each impossible project that's ever been completed, change begins in small segments.

The eradication of rape ultimately hinges on the committed actions of all citizens. Each of us must strive for the resolution of rape. There is an endless range of solutions to the problem of sexual violence when individuals, communities, and churches get involved. The crime can be successfully eliminated when concerned people come together to confront and contest this abomination.

1. National Center for the Prevention and Control of Rape, Room 10C03, Parklawn Building, 5600 Fishers Lane, Rockville, MD 20857.
2. David Finkelhor and Kersti Yllo, *License to Rape* (New York: Holt, Rinehart, and Winston, 1985), p. 201.